CW01081913

Allen & Unwin's House of Books aims to bring
Australia's cultural and literary heritage to a
broad audience by creating affordable print and
ebook editions of the nation's most significant
and enduring writers and their work. The fiction,
non-fiction, plays and poetry of generations of
Australian writers that were published before the
advent of ebooks will now be available to new
readers, alongside a selection of more recently
published books that had fallen out of circulation.

The House of Books is an eloquent collection
of Australia's finest literary achievements.

Georgia Blain has written a number of novels for adults including the bestselling *Closed for Winter*, which was made into a feature film. Her memoir *Births Deaths Marriages: True Tales* was shortlisted for the 2009 Kibble Literary Award for Women Writers.

In 1998 she was named one of the *Sydney Morning Herald*'s Best Young Novelists and has been shortlisted for the NSW Premier's Literary Awards, the SA Premier's Awards and the Barbara Jefferis Award. She lives in Sydney with her partner and daughter.

A&U HOUSE *of* BOOKS

GEORGIA BLAIN

The Blind Eye

This edition published by Allen & Unwin House of Books in 2012
First published by Penguin Books Australia Ltd in 2001

Copyright © Georgia Blain 2001

All rights reserved. No part of this book may be reproduced or
transmitted in any form or by any means, electronic or mechanical,
including photocopying, recording or by any information storage
and retrieval system, without prior permission in writing from the
publisher. The Australian *Copyright Act 1968* (the Act) allows a
maximum of one chapter or 10 per cent of this book, whichever
is the greater, to be photocopied by any educational institution for
its educational purposes provided that the educational institution
(or body that administers it) has given a remuneration notice to
Copyright Agency Limited (CAL) under the Act.

Allen & Unwin
Sydney, Melbourne, Auckland, London

83 Alexander Street
Crows Nest NSW 2065
Australia
Phone: (61 2) 8425 0100
Email: info@allenandunwin.com
Web: www.allenandunwin.com

Cataloguing-in-Publication details are available
from the National Library of Australia
www.trove.nla.gov.au

ISBN 978 1 74331 388 6 (pbk)
ISBN 978 1 74343 084 2 (ebook)

Printed and bound in Australia by the SOS Print + Media Group.

ACKNOWLEDGEMENTS

This book was completed with the assistance of a grant from the Australia Council and a fellowship at the Varuna Writer's Centre. It wouldn't have been possible without the help of both these organisations.

I would like to thank Peter Tuminello, who answered all of my questions about homeopathy with considerable patience. I want to stress that this book is a work of fiction, and that the proving and process of cure I have referred to may differ in some respects from what I believe is the usual practice.

Thanks also to Jinks Dulhunty who gave me access to her library of homeopathic texts. I hung on to them for a long time and hope I haven't returned them in too decrepit a state. I am also very grateful to Rosie Scott, who has always been the mentor that everyone hopes to find. Rosie, Anne Deveson, Andrew Taylor and Peter Bishop from the Varuna Writer's Centre all had the unenviable task of reading earlier drafts and having to tell me the truth. I am grateful for their honesty. Thank you as well to Louise Marsh, who gave me advice on medical matters.

Finally, I also want to thank Fiona Inglis, my agent; Fiona Daniels, who edited the manuscript; and Julie Gibbs, Ali Watts, Sophie Ambrose and everyone else at Penguin who worked very hard in getting this book to its final form.

a true constitution

. . . we have only to rely on the morbid phenomena which the medicines produce in the healthy body as the sole possible revelation of their in-dwelling curative power, in order to learn what disease-producing power, and at the same time, what disease-curing power, each individual medicine possesses.

Samuel Hahnemann, *Organon of Medicine*

~ 1 ~

I, of course, have no idea what it is that we are testing.

There are twelve of us here, including myself, and none of us knows. This blindness, both on the part of the people who will be taking the potential remedy, and the four supervisors (two men, myself and Seamus; and two women, Jeanie and Samantha), is essential if we are to build up a picture of the true nature of the substance we are proving. Any knowledge on our part would only distort each of our responses. You can imagine how it would be. We would not be able to help ourselves. If we heard the word 'venom' whispered, we would immediately begin to suspect our own bodies of displaying the toxicological effects with which we are familiar; we would find ourselves exhibiting a certain expected nature on all levels, the low mean strike of repressed passions spitting forth a venomous poison. Even our dreams would be tainted by all that we bring to that word. Or perhaps it is a plant we know, a mineral, maybe even a diseased tissue that we are testing; in each case we would see what we think we should see, we would bring all that we associate with that substance to this process, and our time would have been wasted.

There is, of course, a director. She is not here with us, but she does know what the remedy is. I met her several times before I decided to leave my practice for a period so that I could take part in this trial. I had been wanting a break, a change in my life, and when I heard of the scale of this particular proving, and the manner in which it would be conducted, I was curious to find out more. But it was not until the director told me the location for the first phase of this experiment, that we would be staying about three hours north of Port Tremaine, that I made up my mind to take part.

She, and the others who work with her, chose this country because the air is dry and the water clean. It is also close to an ideal level above seawater, approximately 400 metres. The food we eat is organic and we are far from the stresses of a hectic urban life. Although the experiment will not be conducted solely in these conditions (it is essential that we also obtain a picture of the remedy within each subject's normal environment), this initial testing will help ensure we get a more reliable set of results than we would otherwise have obtained.

For the first two weeks, the purpose of being here is simply to raise the health of the subjects to as high a level as possible before the dosage is administered. We need to know the nature of each person's true constitution. As part of this process, everyone has been keeping their diaries as instructed, meticulously noting each deviation from their normal state at least three times a day, as well as any possible causes for these changes. This will continue when the provers commence taking the potential remedy (or placebo, in the case of some) and this is when my job will become more demanding. I am meant to monitor my two subjects, to be available for discussion, and to ascertain if and when a dosage should be discontinued. But at this stage I have less to do, and I have had moments of coming close to the quiet I have been craving.

During the days, we walk, write, read and talk, some of us preferring to be with others in the group, some of us wanting to be alone. At night it is cold, a sharp chill that sends us to bed early, so that we wake when the first light reveals a brittle frost across the flatness of the high country, low tufts of grass crunching beneath our feet, each step imprinted dark against silver.

I have been taking time to be by myself, sometimes walking for hours through the prehistoric gorges that surround us, hearing only the sound of my footsteps on the rocks and the occasional cry of a bird in the brilliance of the cloudless blue sky. On other days, I sit out on the verandah that wraps around the house in which we are staying and I look out at the vastness of this land.

The truth is, I have had Silas on my mind. Far more so,

since I came here. But that is hardly surprising, considering our proximity to Port Tremaine and the fact that I ultimately chose to be involved for that very reason. No matter how much you try to guard against it, there are some patients whose stories do not leave you, and the reasons why this occurs may not be ones that you expect, nor may they be particularly rational or readily explicable.

When I stopped at Port Tremaine on my way out here, I wanted to know if Silas had gone back as he had indicated he would the last time I saw him. I also wanted to see it for myself, the town that he had told me about and, more so, the garden in which Rudi and Constance had lived. It had been some years since he had been there, and the differences between what he had described and what I saw could, in certain instances, have been attributed to the passing of time. There was still so much, though, that may never have measured up against the visions he had conjured up for me and the stories he had told.

As I drove away, heading towards the smear of wheat-coloured sky above the darkness of the ranges, and the beginning of my time in this place, I found myself attempting to piece together the fragments of everything I had learnt about him, both from our sessions together and from information I have since obtained elsewhere.

The last time I saw Silas, I told him that an illness returns to its source before cure.

We look to what the very first symptoms were, I explained, *and we are not surprised to find them reappearing as the healing process nears completion. This is the direction that cure takes.*

He had looked away.

I need to go back, he had said.

And although at that stage I had not completely understood the reason why, I had hoped he would meet my eyes, that I would see some realisation of the strength he had found in having reached the point of making such a statement, but he had kept his gaze averted from mine.

— 2 —

It was, in fact, four years ago that Silas first went to Port Tremaine. He was, as he once tried to explain, a different person before that journey. He was like a tight coil that suddenly whipped up from the ground; a whirlwind that took leaves with it in a flurry; a wind that only died to start up again, picking up rubbish this time, a discarded piece of paper, cigarette butts, string, and dying down once more, only to appear seconds later, with no sense or purpose to its path.

He was twenty-four and had never had a job of any consequence. There was no need. He had a trust fund, and access to other sources of wealth that had been carefully secreted away from the authorities' eyes for many years. He came from a family that I had heard of, that most people would have heard of, and although his surname was one that was associated with bankruptcy under dubious circumstances (and with considerable shame), he did not flinch as he spelt it out for the receptionist.

Silas was living in one of his family's apartments at the

time immediately preceding his departure, a huge place that had previously belonged to his grandmother. His parents were in Rome, a city his mother always found stifling in its conservatism, particularly after their years in Barcelona. She would ring late at night, often drunk from several afternoon Camparis, to complain about the expected tedium of that evening's dinner party and to tell him how much she missed him.

If she found him at home, he had usually only just come in, invariably with a group of friends, all of them out of it, and he would put her on speaker phone, so that they could all talk; his enthusiasm for the dinner they'd had, the bar they'd been to, the conversations (or lack of) that had made up the evening, always out of proportion to the reality of the occasion.

She would ask him how Rachel was and he would say that she was fine, everyone laughing now because it had been several months since they had split up, and she would tell him that she was pleased; *put her on, Silas, darling,* and someone would start talking, start pretending to be Rachel, even if they had never met her in the first place.

In those days, he was rarely alone. With more money than he could possibly know how to spend, he found that people gathered around him, aware that he could, and would, provide food, drugs and entertainment for all. Silas knew this, and it never bothered him. He wanted the company, he needed people to affirm his existence; unless, of course, he was in one of those times.

What times? I asked him during one of our earlier sessions together, when we were still laying down the basis from which we could begin to work.

When I was shutting down, when I couldn't bear to see anyone. When the whirlwind died.

And it had a periodicity? I asked.

He did not know what I meant, and I explained. Did it come up regularly, this depression, did it occur at the same given times?

He thought for a moment and told me he wasn't sure. In the case of his slump just prior to his departure, it was his mother's death that had triggered the incident.

But I guess I was heading that way anyway, he said, looking out the window.

Throughout the time he had lived in a different country from his parents, Silas had only maintained contact with his mother. When he heard she had died, he felt, he told me, as though he was without anchor, completely adrift. He stopped answering the phone, he stayed at home by himself, he drank too much, and he took more drugs than usual (*dope, cocaine, whatever,* he explained). A friend of his father's had booked him a ticket to go over to Italy, and although he had intentions of going, at the last minute he changed his mind.

Not consciously, he said. *I just didn't get on the plane.*

When I asked him what eventually prompted him to go to Port Tremaine and make such a radical alteration to his life, Silas told me that he supposed it was a conversation he'd had with a friend of his, Jake.

Jake was a yoga teacher who lived in the apartment building opposite. He and Silas had sex, not often, just sometimes when they ran into each other walking home at night, or heading out on a Saturday morning.

Three weeks after he received the news of his mother's heart attack, Silas saw Jake out on the street. There had been a storm. Hailstones, like oranges, had hurtled out of the sky, pummelling cars and shattering windows, bringing everyone out in its wake. The road was covered in debris, car alarms wailed and people wandered around like spectators at a carnival, amazed by the damage. In the sparkling stillness, Silas just observed the mayhem and breathed in the sweetness of frangipani and lemon-scented gum, flowers and leaves pulverised by the ice.

Jake told him that he looked terrible, which he did.

You could do with a retreat, he suggested and he stretched out on the parquetry floor of Silas's bedroom, legs in the splits, as he reached for his big toe. This was the kind of thing he did after sex, and Silas smiled wryly as he told me that it was one of the reasons why their relationship had never gone any further than it had.

Why don't you get away? His body bent in the other direction. *Take some time out, find out what it's like to be without all this,* and he waved his hand around the room.

It was a throw-away suggestion, but it was one that stuck.

Silas wanted to keep moving, he had to, it was the way in which he survived, and at that stage he would have clung to anything that seemed to hold any possibility of pulling him out of the state he was in.

In the days that followed, he began to toy with the idea. He had received a list of his mother's assets from one of the family's solicitors. It was the value of the house that he noticed first. The solicitor had scrawled a figure, $15 000, followed by a series of question marks next to the brief description, 'four bedrooms, dilapidated'. Silas could not believe anything could be so cheap, and he searched maps for the name of the town.

It was three hours south of the country in which she had grown up, a station that is probably not far from the place where I am staying now. Silas had seen faded black and white photographs of her childhood home -- bleached barren land, country that rolled for miles under flat, hard skies -- and as he traced his finger around the coastline, he read names like Cape Disaster, Desperation Point and then, finally, the far more ordinary Port Tremaine.

He began to spread maps across the floor, splashing red wine across the terrain, conjuring up visions of who he would be, what he would do when he got there, convincing himself that this was a possible direction to take; but more than that, it was the answer to the stultifying emptiness that was threatening to crush him. And, if he hated it, if it was a wrong move, well, he could always just come back. There was nothing to hold him anywhere really.

As Silas told me the story, he glanced up at the clock. In those initial appointments, I could see his discomfort each time we began to discuss Port Tremaine, as well as his desire to talk, both at odds with each other.

I am not a therapist, I told him during our first session, *that is something you should understand. If you feel it's therapy you need, or if you just want to confess all your crimes and misdemeanours, I may not be the person for you.*

He looked away as he shifted in his chair.

It's just that I'm not equipped to guide you in the ways you might be expecting. I knew I needed to be gentle with him, because he was, like so many patients, uncertain as to why he had come and fearful as to what he would find himself revealing. *The help I offer is remedies. Remedies that will hopefully alleviate not only the physical symptoms, but the mental and emotional as well, if that's what you need. In order to choose the remedy, we may have to visit the past, but we will be doing so in a particular way.*

Silas nodded, trying to look as though he understood, as though he had nothing to hide.

In those early days, I was never sure whether we would make any progress. I could see he did not have any faith in what I do (in fact, like most of my patients, he had close to no understanding of the process), but over the years since his return from Port Tremaine, he had found no help from traditional medicine, and he had become, as he admitted reluctantly, somewhat desperate.

As he sketched out his life for me prior to that trip, I was astounded at the hedonistic abandon that had clearly been an integral part of who he was. Not because it shocked me, but because the change that had occurred appeared to be so dramatic.

Even as a child he had never been able to keep still. The numerous nannies who were hired to look after him had usually quit after a couple of weeks. There was a brief period in which his mother had taken him to psychiatrists, all of whom had pronounced him to be precociously bright, somewhat difficult, but quite within the range of normal, and with no relief to be found in their verdicts, she had decided to just accept the way he was. If the nannies threatened to quit, she offered them a raise. When that didn't work, there was always another who would take the job (particularly with its accompanying salary). If Silas had too much energy, well, there was no point fighting it, and she took to bringing him down from his room for dinner-party guests, his wild dancing to any music they chose to play always a sure source of entertainment, particularly after they'd had a few drinks. And as he got older, there were the boarding schools.

Eight by the time I was sixteen, he admitted.

Why? I asked.

He looked out the window as he listed his sins: selling drugs, sex in the dormitories, refusing to participate in sport; he was even an instigator in a Gay Pride rally despite having no clear sexual preference. *Just the usual stuff,* he told me.

His parents finally found an experimental school that was willing to take him.

The School Without Walls.

I smiled as he told me the name. I knew it. I had been there myself, three years earlier.

Similar sins, I told Silas, unable to hide the glimmer of amusement in my eyes as I remembered the way in which I, too, had rebelled, shortly after my mother was first hospitalised with depression, and how my father, an analyst, believed that the answer was more freedom, rather than less.

It was at that moment that Silas decided he would attempt to trust me, despite the misgivings he'd had on first entering the building and seeing the tenants listed at the entrance: aura readers, psychic healers and colour therapists.

As he shifted in his chair and looked around the consulting room, he told me he wanted this to work, he needed it to work, and I promised him I would do all I could to help.

— 3 —

Silas had been living with the way he was for three years before he saw me. Looking back, I do not know how he did it.

As I sit outside in the brightness of the morning sun remembering our conversations, I can hear the others packing a picnic lunch and I know I will soon have to join them. I have found myself becoming increasingly antisocial (not just here, but in life generally, although at home this trend is less obvious than it is in a place such as this where I have to live with others), and I do not know how to reverse this process, or if, in fact, I even have the will to attempt it.

Are you working on something? Hamish asked me this morning. He is one of the provers and he has been encouraging everyone to do yoga with him in the morning, refusing to give up on those of us who promise him we will be out there on the verandah with him in the freezing cold, just not today, not this particular dawn, but tomorrow.

He wanted to know whether I was writing a new text, and I told him I was simply using the time as space in which to think, that it was something I had been craving.

I guess it must get draining, treating people, he said.

Not really. It was an automatic response, and as I uttered it I realised there was no need to lie. I smiled at him. *Actually, it does.*

I had never expected the degree of exhaustion that I would experience in full-time consulting, and this is not to say that I do not enjoy my work. I am lucky, I have found what is right for me. Six months into my medical degree, I stumbled upon this field and switched courses, despite considerable advice to the contrary. Suddenly, I had discovered a whole new way of looking at the world, and at the end of my studies I was eager to begin practising. I wanted to heal, I still do; it is just that sometimes the weight of other lives, the intensity of the process that is necessary with each and every patient, can be overwhelming, and I was ill-prepared. In my eagerness to make a difference, I took on too much. Worse still, I am, for various reasons, a person who finds it difficult to mark off where responsibility for another should end. I manage, but I am only just coming to realise the price I have paid, and despite my repeated vows to remedy the situation, I have done nothing about it until now.

Silas once told me that he had often spent weeks completely alone. After his return from Port Tremaine, he did not, in fact, see anyone for over a month; he just stayed in his apartment, with all the curtains drawn. Finally he stepped outside into the warmth of the late summer sunshine and walked to the street corner, uncertain as to what to do with himself when he got there. He stood for an hour, watching the old ladies with their immaculate hair and too-bright lipstick walking their tiny dogs, the junkies arguing with each other, the council workers sweeping the previous night's refuse into piles, the heated exchange between a waitress and a young man who had ordered his coffee over ten minutes ago; all of it spread out, distant and unreal, in front of him.

That was when he saw Rachel. As she hurried across the street, tiny, thin, her mouth brilliant red in the paleness of her face, he remembered when he had thought he was in love with her, the brief time when he would have done anything for her, and he called out her name, without thinking.

She was surprised to see him. She had heard he'd been away, some impossibly small town somewhere, and he told her the name of the place, knowing it would mean nothing to her.

For godsakes, why did you go and do that? she laughed.

I don't know, he said, and he didn't. He had no idea why he had done anything he had done.

She looked at him, concerned for a moment, but she was in a hurry, he could see that, and any vision he'd had of them talking now seemed foolish. Rachel, and everyone else he had known from the time they had been together, belonged to a life that had gone; they could have no place in his existence as it was now.

Give me a call, she said. *You look like you need to get out.*

And he tried to sound convincing as he promised her he would.

— 4 —

The image you have of a place when you see it on a map rarely concords with the reality that confronts you when you arrive.

I had heard Silas's descriptions of Port Tremaine so I had an idea of what the town would be like when I first turned off the highway in the direction indicated by the sign, but he had nothing to help him build a picture of what he would find. It was a holiday place, he supposed: beaches, old shacks, a milk bar selling ice-creams, a house where he would paint, maybe write, perhaps just lie around and read; it didn't matter. Now that he had decided this was what he wanted to do, he was determined that it would be amazing, incredible, something he should have done years ago, and that was how he would envisage it.

He drove for two days with Tess Davis in the passenger seat next to him. After three nights of toasting his departure, she had been the last one left at his apartment, and the next morning he had talked her into getting in the car with him. *Come on,* he had urged, *throw caution to the wind,* not wanting to recognise that somewhere, deep inside, he was scared; and, still drunk, she had finally just shrugged her shoulders and grinned: *why the fuck not?*

As the country became increasingly barren, desert brush and prickly pear stretching flat before them, the sky unrelentingly blue overhead, they talked less and less. Driving past abandoned roadside stalls, collapsed signs promising cheap flowers, vegetables, fruit, one kilometre away, five hundred metres and then, there at the promised site, nothing, they passed a joint back and forth without a word.

I think I want to go home, she eventually said when they pulled up at a service station near the entrance to the gulf, the water a dirty grey on the horizon.

With the car door open an inch, Silas could feel the blanket of dry heat hovering still around him, breathtaking in its ferocity.

It's not far, he urged. *Look at it,* and he waved his arm, trying to indicate how extraordinary it was, not wanting to look at her, not wanting to see the realisation of where she was in her eyes.

There was a bus station two kilometres back along the road and he drove her there, gave her some money and told her he'd write. She just stared at him in disbelief.

Aren't you going to wait with me? she asked.

He hadn't wanted to. He feared that if he stopped he wouldn't go on. He was also so stoned that he hadn't even thought of the obvious, that it probably wasn't okay to just leave her on the highway. They sat in the car with all the doors open, hoping to catch a breeze from the gulf but none came. Thick clusters of flies clung to their faces, their legs, their arms, barely moving when they tried to flick them away. Silas would have just given up on them, but Tess kept brushing at them, her hands occasionally slapping against his neck or his cheek in her attempts to get them out of the car. He was close to the point of hitting her back when he finally saw the bus, its metal roof shimmering in the distance.

There it is, and the sudden volume of Tess's voice made him jump.

She was out of the car immediately, waving her arms in the air, not wanting to risk even the slightest possibility that it would go past without stopping, barely looking at him in her eagerness to get away, her fare in one sweaty hand, her bag in the other. As the doors clanged shut behind her, she did not even turn to wave.

See you, Silas called out to the departing bus.

As he watched her go, he caught a glimpse of his face in the rear-vision mirror, tired, his eyes bloodshot, the sweat trickling through the dirt on his forehead, and he was surprised that he was still where he was, there by the side of the road in the long hard heat of the afternoon.

Silas drove that last four hours with the radio off, the sun slowly sinking as he passed derelict buildings, golden in the afternoon light, some no more than walls crumbling into the sandy soil, others more recently deserted, pubs with doors barred shut, empty houses with gardens choked by thistles, boarded-up shops, their signs faded and rusty.

He pulled over at the turn-off to Port Tremaine and looked behind him at the last of the light hitting the ranges in the distance, the dark red now faded to a dusky mauve, the slopes flecked with trees, tufts of olive against the purple. It was cooler now and he could finally feel a slight breeze from the gulf as he rolled another joint and drank the last of the bottle of water Tess had left on the floor. He lit the joint and got out of the car.

This was country that had been decimated. I know, I saw it. Lured by months of surprisingly good rainfall, the settlers who first went there had thought it would be rich land, farming country where wheat would grow, golden and strong, but as years passed and the rain failed to return, they realised they had been fooled. Those who stayed were left with nothing but a memory of what might have been, in a place that proved far harsher than they would ever have believed.

As Silas walked across the paddock, the dry grasses scratching his ankles, he saw the great ravines that rip across the land, the surrounding soil collapsing in upon itself, cake-like. He touched the edge of a mound of dirt with his toe and watched it crumble, dirty yellow, revealing another inch of tree roots beneath his feet, and he traced them back with his eye to where it stood, the only tree in sight.

Fifty kilometres to Port Tremaine. That was all. He could see the faded black paint on the sign and he knew it would take him no more than twenty minutes to get there. It was not going to be the seaside village he had envisaged, there was no point in pretending otherwise, and he ground the last of the joint into the dirt and headed back to the car.

the first consultation

⎯⎯

. . . case-taking is an art. The interviewer can be compared to a painter who slowly and painstakingly brings forth an image which represents in its essence a particular vision of reality.

George Vithoulkas, *The Science of Homeopathy*

— 1 —

I have to at least try to be honest with myself; I have to at least admit that my preoccupation with Silas is not just due to the fact that he was a patient I found particularly interesting, it is also because he was responsible for bringing Greta back into my life. Because the truth is, each time I remember him, I am also drawn back to her, and I flinch, uncomfortable with her renewed presence in my consciousness, unable to leave it alone, yet still not knowing how to make peace with this particular aspect of my past.

I knew her over ten years ago (I was twenty-one at the time, and so very different to the way I am now), and I did not know her for long. But she was, I suppose, a turning point in my life. Sometimes I wonder whether all that happened between us marked the line between the person I once was and the person I became, which is not to say that I took a completely unexpected path; I didn't. I already knew I wanted to do this kind of work, that it was right for me, I was already the type to throw myself in with too much intensity. After Greta there was, however, a fear, an anxiety about failing others that grew, creeping, dark and intangible, at the back of all I said and did, tempering me, constricting me, never letting me forget its presence.

When Silas first mentioned Greta's name to me, I did my best not to react. It was, in fact, right at the beginning of our first appointment. I asked him who had referred him and he told me that it was someone he had only recently met.

Greta, he said, *Greta Sorenson.*

And I wrote her name down in the appropriate space on the form, without glancing in his direction.

He had sat behind her in the reading room of the State Library for three months before they talked. Later, she told me that she had found it curious that he always picked the seat directly behind hers. Wherever she was sitting, he would follow, seeming to choose her as a marker, as some kind of stable point in the enormity of that room, without ever really being aware of her existence. As far as she knew, he never did anything. Occasionally he had a book open in front of him and, even more rarely, she would hear him take out a piece of paper and pen, but most of the time he just sat there.

Greta was researching the life of a little-known sculptor for an academic. When I saw her again, shortly before I came out here, she told me that work such as this, along with brief stints in galleries and the odd hours in art-supply shops, was how she earned a living. She didn't enjoy research (it was the solitude that she found difficult), but it was far better paid than most of the other jobs she could get, and she had begun to find a certain pleasure in taming a life into a neat row of categories, her pages ruled into columns with headings such as 'Work', 'Travel' and 'Love' marked across the top.

Sometimes she would catch herself leaning backwards, trying to see what Silas was doing. Other times, when he went out for a cigarette, she would get a little bolder, turning right around in an attempt to find some clue as to who he was, but the only thing he ever wrote was the beginning of a letter, the same two words scrawled across the page – *Dear Rudi* – only to be crossed out, and then repeated, over and over again.

She was sitting on the front steps, her back warm in the early autumn sunshine, when they first spoke. He asked her if she had a light.

He told her his name and took the step below her, cupping his hands over the end of his cigarette as he tried to stop the match from blowing out.

Greta was never shy with people she did not know. She was, in fact, at her best with strangers, disarmingly attractive in her ability to strike up a conversation with someone she had only just met, and she grinned as she looked at Silas and told him that she had wondered when he was finally going to speak to her. *I've been curious about you,* she explained, and she asked him what it was that he did.

Nothing, he told her, aware of how strange his answer sounded. *I guess I've just been thinking.*

In the glare of sunlight bouncing off an office block, his eyes were dark green; hazel when he turned away.

About anything in particular?

He shook his head and traced the tip of his cigarette along the edge of the step. *What about you?*

She told him about the project she was working on, and the academic who had employed her. *She is trying to prove that this woman was at the forefront of a particular artistic movement, that she was an unrecognised great. The problem is, her work was fairly ordinary.*

She took out a photo to show him and he smiled as he looked at the piece. *It doesn't look too flash,* he agreed.

Greta's phone rang, and as she searched for it in her bag, Silas stubbed out his cigarette and raised a hand in farewell. She watched him, tall and thin, taking the stairs two at a time as he made his way back to the entrance, and she thought it was strange that he always wore a jumper, the sleeves never pushed up, even though it was still warm.

They soon found out that they lived only a couple of streets away from each other and they began to leave at the same time, either walking across the rapidly darkening parklands together, or catching the train. I can only guess as to what they would have talked about, I can only take the pieces that I know and join them myself, but this is the way it will have to be if I am to form a coherent whole.

She would have told him that she had been brought up by her grandparents in the country, that she had moved to the city when she was seventeen, and that she wanted to live in New York.

Just for a while. Just to see if I can.

She wanted to be a curator. She was not good enough to be an artist herself, she had learnt that a long time ago, and she would have smiled slightly as she told him that she wanted to work overseas because she had a constant need to test herself, to push beyond the boundaries of the safe worlds she knew. Leaving the country town where she had grown up had been the first step. Going to New York was the next. But it was not just geographical boundaries, and she would have laughed; she had a tendency to push herself to the limit in all she experienced. She would have blushed then as she realised she had once again revealed too much, only to find that he had not told her anything about himself; in fact, after several days of walking home together, she would have to admit she knew no more about him than she had on the first day they had talked.

Despite this, she still slept with him, only three weeks after they met. I do not know whether she did so hoping she would get to know him more, that this would be the start of a relationship, but I would guess so. Most of us want to be loved. Some of us go to extraordinary lengths to hide this need, others of us have it on display, naked and awkward. Greta was always looking for the person who would save her, who would love her enough to make everything all right, and she was always disappointed.

As she and Silas had been about to part on the usual corner, he had stopped her. She was surprised when he had suggested a drink, when he had suddenly seemed to want to be a part of the early evening, the street lights flickering on overhead, the rush of people heading home carrying food and flowers, the bars opening their doors, and she had followed him across the street and down the back alley.

His footsteps were loud in the lobby as, some hours later, they both stumbled into his apartment building, arm in arm. She saw herself in the elevator mirror and she hated the flush across her cheeks, the haziness in her eyes, and the lurid orange of her mouth under the fluorescent light, but then he was kissing her, his lips moving up to her ear; *Greta, Greta, Greta,* he whispered, and she knew he was drunk too as he dropped his keys twice at the entrance to his flat. That was when she remembered that she had meant to finish writing up the first part of her notes, but she just thought *fuck it*, this was what she wanted, and as she felt the brush of his lips on her neck as he led her through to the bedroom, there was a moment when he seemed about to say something, but she didn't let him because, whatever it was, she was pretty certain she didn't want to know.

In the soft light of the next morning, Greta sat opposite Silas and wondered why she hadn't just gone, grabbed her bag in the middle of the night and gone. She supposed she had been so confused, so uncertain as to whether what was happening was in fact happening, that she had been unable to act. But that was not all there was to it; she had also been worried about leaving him alone.

Now, sober and exhausted, she was scared, wanting only to leave, but feeling that she had to somehow go through the motions of attempting to talk.

Do you have any idea what you did? she asked him. Her mouth was dry from the alcohol and cigarettes and she did not want to look at him because she did not want to see him for what he really was: a stranger.

He did not answer and she glanced at the wounds he had been cutting into his arms when she had found him, there on the kitchen floor, alone in the darkness. He was watching her and his eyes were black in the paleness of his face. He looked away.

Has it happened before? She did not know why she wanted to cry and she bit her lip.

He told her it had.

Often?

A couple of times a month.

The intimacy of having had sex was close and raw enough. Attempting to have this conversation was too much for either of them.

Why? And her voice was small as she shook her head. *You should have warned me,* and she was aware of the ludicrousness of her comment as soon as she made it.

He smiled for the first time that morning, the expression on his crooked mouth sheepish as he told her it wouldn't have been much of an enticement in getting her up to his place. *I hoped it wouldn't happen,* he said. *I really did.*

As she rubbed at the sleep in the corners of her eyes, she said she thought he needed to get some help.

He had already tried; he had been to psychiatrists, to doctors, there had been meditation, naturopathic treatments, diet, acupuncture, and as he listed each attempt he had made, she just wrote down my name, *Daniel Lehaine,* and the place where she'd heard I had my practice.

She reached for her bag. From his kitchen window, she would have been able to see how the sky stretched, soft blue, over the impossible perfection of the day. The first autumn leaves would have floated past, and with the sun behind them, they would have shone, translucent.

She kissed him awkwardly, wishing she hadn't as soon as the moment passed, and she told him she would see him around.

Later, when I asked her why she had sent him to me, I was surprised by her answer.

She smiled. *He reminded me of you.*

Really? I asked her, trying to keep my voice level.

Not what you are now, she told me. *What you were then.*

— 2 —

Port Tremaine has a main street and five back streets that make up the grid of the town. Only the main street is bitumen; the rest are dirt, eventually petering out into either the surrounding scrub or the mangrove swamps that border the gulf.

Silas could remember it all in sharp detail. He could mark each house and tell you whether it was deserted or occupied, and if it was occupied, who lived in it. He could tell you which of the businesses still opened their doors to customers and which were boarded up, the owners having long since given up on any hope of surviving in a town that depended on a country now laid bare and empty, stretched out, silent and wasted, beneath the vastness of the sky.

He even told me about the giant palms, their growth stunted by the tyres around the base of their trunks; they sit, squat and ugly along the centre of the main street, like discarded overgrown pineapples. It is a street that stretches down to a jetty, the jetty reaching for over a kilometre into the still, silvery waters of the gulf. Built to accommodate a tide that sucks out and out, leaving tiny crabs scurrying across the sand and clumps of weed drying to a salty crisp under the harsh glare of the sun, the length of that jetty is the only claim to fame the town has.

In the searing heat of the long summer days, it is usually deserted. There may be one or two locals who are out there, or perhaps the occasional fisherman who has turned off the highway to spend a slow and lazy afternoon leaning over the railing, line dangling, bait at his feet, but most of the time it is empty. The streets are also bare, just a few chickens scratching around in the dirt to indicate any sign of life, and nothing else.

Once a working port, there were over 600 people living there in the early 1900s. The grain was brought down through the Port Tremaine Gorge and loaded onto the boats to be shipped off to the rest of the world. When Silas arrived, the port had long since closed and the town had dwindled to sixty residents, including Rudi and Constance, although most of Port Tremaine would not consider them in any head count. Silas could name many of them; he could describe what they looked like, where they lived and what they did. He later told me that occasionally their faces would float across the slow beginnings of a dream, and he would start, waking suddenly with the fear that he was back there once more.

The sign at the entrance marks the population as 240, but

it is, of course, many years out of date, and with numbers continuing to drop so steadily there has never been any point in regularly changing it. Silas saw it in the beam of the headlights as he slowed down, knowing he had hit the top of the main road, the four street lights pale in the darkness. There was only one other car out, its engine at a low throb as it cruised down to where the jetty began, the driver revving the accelerator for a minute or so, before turning and proceeding at the same slow pace, back to the other end of town.

Unsteady on his feet, and slightly nauseous from lack of food and too much dope, Silas got out at the first pub he came across, not even noticing how dark and quiet it was until he was there at the front door and he realised it was closed. Each window was shut, tattered canvas blinds were pulled down, the glass in the front door was smashed and boarded up with chipboard, the sign on the front advertised counter meals with prices he had not seen for years.

He stood in the middle of the deserted street and smelt the salt in the air. After the heat of the day, the gulf breeze was cool on the clamminess of his forehead and he looked down to where the jetty began, relieved to see that there was another pub, one that appeared to be open.

That was when he noticed the old man, head down, an almost empty bottle in one hand, his entire body concentrated on getting another drink, his face hidden by long grey hair that fell to below his shoulder blades. He was talking to himself, muttering into his beard, words that Silas could not hear as he followed him towards the hotel, eventually finding himself close enough to smell the sweet alcoholic sweat on the old man's skin as he pushed the bar door open, letting it swing shut behind him with a thud, so that it almost closed in Silas's face.

In the dim light of the vast room, Silas saw the few men clustered at the counter turn away as the old man took a seat and fumbled for coins in his pocket, only to turn back again seconds later when they saw Silas enter. All eyes were on Silas now, and in that moment he knew they all wanted to know who this person was, this person who was foolish enough to come to a town that everyone had left.

— 3 —

Dear Rudi

Sitting at his reading desk, Silas would press his knuckles into his eyes, wanting the world to swim momentarily, wanting to see the swirl of colours that filled his vision before the darkness took over. This, he once told me, was what he did with his days.

He had his notepad open in front of him, each page covered with those two words, and next to it were the books he had discovered when he first came to the library. Kirlian photography, a technique for capturing the electromagnetic field that surrounds every living object. Leaves represented by flares of orange, red, violet; one finger touching another, the colours deep and dark except at the point of contact, a brilliant yellow glowing between them; a dying flower; the image of where a petal had been just prior to the moment when it was plucked; that was how the field appeared.

He would look up at Greta there in front of him, her head bent over a box of letters from her sculptor's tutor to his lover, and as he stared at the part in her hair, a crooked white zigzag between the paleness of her plaits, he would wonder what the colours were that surrounded her.

Dear Rudi

Those two words. Crossed out for the twentieth time that morning.

— *4* —

It took Silas six weeks to get his first appointment with me. Unfortunately, this is the way it is with most of us who prac- tise in this field, the length of individual consultations making it impossible for any of us to take on many new patients.

I am sorry, the receptionist told him, as she tells most people who ring, *if it's urgent, I can try and squeeze you in a little earlier, but it must be urgent.*

Because he had been living with the way he was for such a long time, it was difficult now to describe his need as urgent. Silas told her it was okay, he would wait. But once the time was booked, the turnover of days began to slow and he wished he had said he was desperate.

Each day that he saw Greta at the library, he wanted to talk to her, but the few attempts he made were awkward, and he did not know what to say to change what had hap- pened. When he told her he had made the appointment but the waiting list was over a month, she said she was sorry there was nothing she could do to push it along.

It's just that I don't really know him anymore.

He was about to walk away, but she stopped him, finding it hard to meet his eyes as she told him we had been in a relationship some time ago. We met before she went to art school, when we were both at the College of Healing, and as she spoke she realised that she had made this revelation in the hope of returning to the ease with which she and Silas had originally conversed.

I was never going to finish, I was never any good at it, she said and smiled, embarrassed, but glad he had stopped.

Later, when Silas told me that it was Greta who had referred him, I wondered for a moment whether I should find out more about his relationship with her, and whether I should, in fact, refer him to someone else. I glanced at my notes and saw that he had already been waiting six weeks. I looked across at him and saw the anxiety in his eyes, and I decided against it.

I told him that the first appointment would be a little different to those that would follow. It would be longer, for one thing. It would involve a lot of questions, questions that might seem irrelevant, but that would help me in seeing the total picture.

I asked him why he had come and he attempted to explain a burning sensation in his heart, a tightness that would wring the breath out of him, leaving him crippled with pain.

Anything else?

Silas shook his head. He could not speak of the wounds he inflicted upon himself, despite the fact that this was the real reason for the visit. This is the way it often is with patients; the process of bringing out the core of the problem is not a quick one. For Silas, the memory of Greta's face the morning after she had stayed the night was still fresh and the shame he felt made him glance at the ground.

The questions that I asked were fairly standard: Silas's like or dislike of various weather conditions and whether he noted an aggravation of symptoms in wind, rain, damp, heat; whether they changed according to the time of day, morning, night; his appetite and whether he had any particular food cravings or aversions . . . Silas answered everything despite not being able to see the point.

What about sex? My gaze was direct and he did not attempt to meet it.

What about it?

Tell me a bit about your sex life, your desire, the frequency with which you have it.

He said he didn't have sex often at the moment. Greta was, in fact, the only person he had slept with in a year, and as he told me this I could see he was uncertain as to whether he should have mentioned it.

It's fine, I assured him, and he looked relieved.

I paused for a moment in my note-taking, sipping the

water in the glass next to me, in the hope of creating a space that he would fill with words, but Silas kept silent.

So, and I smiled, *how about your general energy?*

It was low, Silas said, and he shifted uncomfortably in his chair.

What about your relationships with other people?

He did not know what I meant. He was not in a relationship with anyone, he hadn't been in one for a long time.

I told him that I was talking in a more general sense; I wanted to know about his family, his friends.

He said that his mother was dead, and his father, from whom he had been estranged, had also died a year ago. *I suppose I spend most of my time alone,* and he looked out the window at the plumbing from the opposite building, the rusted pipes the only possible distraction from the intensity of the interview.

I could see that the facts of his life, laid bare like this, did not seem as though they belonged to him, and I waited for a moment before I asked my next question.

It was sleep I wanted to know about, and as Silas opened his mouth to reply, his face blanched. It was the tightness in his chest, the constriction, ferocious enough to render him incapable of answering.

How is it? Fitful? Deep, disturbed, any regular dreams, night wakings, difficulties going to sleep, waking up?

It took me an instant to see that he was in pain, and the moment I did, I reached for him, my hand on his sleeve as

I told him to breathe, it would be all right, it would pass. As he leant forward, I tried to get him to meet my eyes.

Slowly, Silas sat up. He touched the spot where I had been holding him, gently, carefully. I could still feel it, the burning tightness there in my hand.

So that's the pain? I asked.

Silas nodded.

~ 5 ~

I saw the pub that Silas stayed in when he first got to Port Tremaine. It was, surprisingly, still open for business despite being completely deserted. I remember calling out, hoping to find someone to whom I could talk, but no one answered. I waited for a moment, and then decided that I would keep going. I wanted to make it out to Rudi's garden and back before the chill of the evening, and if I had no luck there, I would try to find the owner later.

Silas told me he spent his first two days in that town crashed out, sweaty and exhausted, finally waking to find himself in a room that was, as the owner had promised, suffering from the fact that it had been uninhabited for some time.

He remembered a woman called Martha bringing him a set of sheets, worn with a faded cornflower print, a single blanket, a pillow with a cigarette burn that went through to the stuffing, and a threadbare towel. When he woke, they were all where she had left them, there at the end of the bed. He had slept fully clothed on the mattress, unaware that night had passed to day and back to night again.

Walking down the main street, with the address of his mother's house written on a scrap of paper, he saw, as I also did, the extent of the desolation. At first glance it appears like a perfectly preserved country town, the stone buildings golden in the brilliance of the sunshine, the awnings shading the footpath; but where you would expect to find people resting out of the heat, talking to neighbours they have known for years, it is empty, always empty. It was, Silas once said, like being in a Western. All of the shops, apart from Pearl's General Store and the garage across the street, were deserted, the displays faded in the windows, the plastic grass in the butcher's no longer a brilliant green but the true yellow of the country, the shelves at the back of the haberdasher's still stacked with bolts of cloth, rotten to the touch, some doors creaking open, others locked with 'Keep Out' scrawled across in red paint, the rooms beyond ransacked, even the floorboards pulled up, leaving nothing but an empty rotten shell.

It was Pearl who had told him that the house was on the sea front. Finding the pub empty when he woke, he had gone to her in search of food. The chips he had bought were so stale as to be inedible, and as he scattered them to the gulls, he noted the dilapidation of each place he passed and braced himself for what he would find.

From the gate, he could see a caravan with 'Tricia's Treasures' painted on the side, the house beyond slowly crumbling into the garden, the caravan itself leaning lop-sided into a ravine. He could only presume that someone had squatted there, and he struggled to push the gate open, the pathway beyond almost completely overgrown, the weeds sticking to his calves as he made his way towards it. When he peered through the ruffled daisy curtains, he saw clothes still hanging on the racks, sheets on the bed, dishes in the sink, all coated with fine yellow dirt. The cactus garden that bordered the track to the house was overrun with prickly pear. Tiny bleached bones that looked like they belonged to rats or feral cats crunched beneath his feet as he hastened away, past the unused well now choked with brambles, and up to the deserted building beyond. His mother's house.

There was a bath. It was out the back in the open air, and over one end was draped a flannel. It looked as though it had just been used, as though the person who lived there had just gone, wanting only to get out of the place, not caring what was left behind, and for one moment Silas wondered whether he was, in fact, intruding.

Suddenly uneasy, he ran back down the path, over the bones, the gate falling off its hinges as he opened it, the rust staining his hands, his breath short as he stumbled onto the emptiness of the road.

He had no idea why he had come to this place. He sat in the gutter and wondered at the strangeness of owning a house that meant nothing to him. It must have been where his mother had gone for holidays when she was young. He could not imagine her as a child; he could only see her as his mother, always adoring, always in a slightly inebriated haze, the ash from her cigarette crumbling into her drink as she pressed him close and recounted his latest antics to whoever happened to be there for lunch.

It was his father who had done the deal, selling off the station and all its holdings shortly after his grandfather's death. Somehow this place must have slipped through the net. He looked back at it. This was to have been his project. That's what Silas had told his friends, and he had painted a picture of a rambling seaside home where they could all come and stay, anyone, anytime.

I, too, saw the house and I smiled to myself as I remembered how Silas had recounted picking himself up from the gutter, wiping the grit from his hands, determined to convince himself that it was not impossible, no, not impossible at all.

What a place, Silas told Pearl, standing by the cool of the refrigerator.

Not the way it always was, and she shook her head as she peered at him through her thick glasses, taking his measure, up and down, with an unfaltering stare.

But not completely irretrievable.

She just grunted in reply.

Crossing the road in front of her shop, he saw Mick at the entrance to the garage. *I'm Silas,* he said, trying not to step on the tools that littered the floor of the workshop.

They clasped hands, awkwardly, and he could see the question – Silas, what kind of a fuckin' name is that? – there on Mick's face.

Stayin' a while?

Think so, he told Mick, as he would tell everyone who asked.

He could hear his own footsteps as he walked the streets, peering into empty buildings, trying to see through the gap in the curtains, the rip in the blind, fascinated by the extent of the desertion, and he began to walk a little faster, down towards the jetty, not wanting to admit that he felt strangely vulnerable by himself, as though he were being watched. It might have been that car he had seen on the first night, slowly circling the back streets, leaving a trail of dust in its path, the windows wound up high, the engine a deep throttle, slowing down as it approached him, passing in a cloud of smoke and then nearing closer again, this time from another direction, another road.

Just Steve, Thai said when he asked her about it later. She was wiping the snot from the nose of her youngest child with the back of her hand.

She had a cottage at the rear of her place. Martha had told him about it when he had returned to the pub at the end of the day. She was microwaving a plate of grey roast lamb in the cavernous pub kitchen, built for an era long past. He had looked at the food longingly because, unappetising as it had appeared to be, he had not eaten for two days, and as she sat and ate it in front of him, he had asked her if she knew of anywhere he could stay for a while.

Matt and Thai Wilde. End of the main street and turn left.

There had been no need to give further directions, even a street number. Theirs was the only occupied place on the block, right next to his mother's in fact, the front yard littered with chickens, broken-down cars and rusted toys, a parched vegetable garden out the back and, beyond that, the single-roomed house that Silas could have for five dollars a night, ten if he wanted food.

Saw you walkin' round, Thai said when he came to ask her about the room.

When she grinned, he saw that she had probably once been attractive. He watched as she brought in the washing, her still-taut body visible beneath the batik dress she wore, and he wondered what she would be like to sleep with.

When he offered to help her, she looked at him like he was mad. She had the transistor radio propped up on the verandah steps and, unable to maintain any semblance of stillness, he picked up the youngest child, a girl who was only just beginning to walk, and danced her round the clothesline.

Where the fuck do you get your energy from? Thai asked.

Silas dipped the child down low and deposited her into the basket of dry clothes. *Don't know,* he grinned. *I was born with it.*

But eventually the heat got to even him, and early that evening after dumping his belongings in his room, he walked out into the stillness of the gulf, his body drained by the fierceness of the sun. The sand was cool beneath his feet as the water lapped against his ankles, licked his calves, and seemed to progress no further until, far from the shoreline, the slow lick finally reached his knees, his thighs, his waist, and at last, he could submerge himself. Taking another joint out of the plastic in which he had wrapped it, he floated on his back, and that town, with its decrepit buildings and, behind them, the darkness of the ranges, was a surreal vision.

Incredible, he whispered to himself, momentarily aware that he couldn't remember the last time he hadn't been stoned.

the field

The first striking evidence of electromagnetic fields associated with the human body came not from research but from observations of unusual cases in which the field was exaggerated beyond normal experience:

Perhaps the most impressive of these cases was that of a fourteen-year-old girl in Missouri, who, in 1895, suddenly seemed to turn into an electrical dynamo. When reaching for metal objects such as a pump handle her fingertips gave off sparks of such high voltage that she actually experienced pain. So strong was the electricity coursing through her body that a doctor who attempted to examine her was actually knocked onto his back, where he remained unconscious for several seconds. To the young lady's relief, her ability to shock eventually began to diminish and had vanished completely by the time she was twenty.

Quoted in S Krippner and D Rubin (eds),
The Kirlian Aura,
reproduced in George Vithoulkas,
The Science of Homeopathy

— *1* —

I am wary of being consumed by my own thoughts, my memories of Silas and all that I associate with him. I have been trying to make more of an effort to spend time with the others and not just be on my own but as each day progresses, I invariably find I have drifted off by myself, yet again.

Jeanie, one of the other supervisors, has brought her cattle dog, Sam, with her and Sam seems to have become my main companion. On our third day here, I took a burr out of her paw. I had seen her limping down the path that leads to the wood shed, and I ignored her growls as I took her leg in my hand and felt the soft pads of her feet. Since then, she has taken to sleeping on the end of my bed and coming for walks with me, some misshapen stick always gripped in her mouth. The hopeful expression on her face is always enough to make me relent and throw it for her even though I know that if I give in once, she will be still more persistent, dropping it at my feet every few metres.

She normally doesn't like people, Jeanie told me last night as she watched Sam stretching, preparing to follow me up to my room. *Maybe she senses that you've become even more of a loner than she has,* and she looked at me quizzically before turning back to her crossword.

Conscious of her comment, and slightly shamed by it, I tried a little harder this evening, staying up with some of the others to play a game of Scrabble by the fire. In the brief time we have been here, people have already begun to relax with each other; tonight there were even some joking attempts at guessing what it is that everyone will be taking. Neither I nor the other supervisors should, strictly speaking, encourage this, and the others knew it, grinning at me shame-faced as I told them their guesses were as good as mine.

The truth is we could be testing any substance, absolutely anything, and that is because everything has within it the possibility of producing a wide spectrum of varied symptoms, and hence of being used in treatment. Conversely, it is also possible to poison using any substance, provided it is given in sufficient quantities; even the most everyday foods, such as salt or starch, can be toxic if they are given in large doses over a long period of time.

Obviously, the testing we will be doing is not crude. If a substance is administered in toxic doses, we will see a reaction, but what we see will probably be of little use in later treatment. What we want is the finer picture: the highly refined and specific symptoms that are produced when minute doses are taken. This is what will allow us to determine the resonant frequency at which this particular substance vibrates. The people who are here must therefore be capable of describing the most subtle changes that occur in each plane – the physical, emotional and mental. That is what they will need to record in their diaries.

Sitting at the kitchen table, Larissa and Matthew (the two provers I will be supervising) are writing up their notes. Every so often one of them pauses and looks up at the ceiling. They are searching for the word they want. It is an intense form of self-examination, and in a small group like this, such continual navel-gazing could have its problems. We all know this and we are careful, because each and every one of us has a faith in this process and a belief in its importance.

Rudi Weiss often wrote about the power of a common faith in holding a community together. When Silas first mentioned his name to me, I did not tell him that I had actually heard of him, that he had been one of my heroes when I was a student. I had read about the alternative lifestyle he and a dozen or so others had established on the outskirts of Port Tremaine over thirty years ago. They had wanted a community that was sustainable, one that was based on respect for each other and for the land on which they lived. I was inspired by their work, and I am not just talking about the developments they made in the process of cure.

These articles were all written some time ago. I did not know what had happened to their group until I met Silas and learnt that there was only Rudi and his daughter, Constance, left out there. The others had gone. It was, like so many small utopian communities, a place that lasted for a while and then, for reasons I can only guess at, disintegrated rapidly. Perhaps our own faith, our own belief is not always enough; we need others to confirm the visions we create for ourselves if we are to have any hope of sustaining them.

$\sim$ *2* $\sim$

Silas told me that it was Thai who always did the rolling.

It was her thing.

She would lick the paper flat and twist the end with a business-like efficiency; small, skinny joints, one for each of them.

She had guessed he was loaded, and when she had asked him if he could spare a little, *to get her through the day*, he had shown her the stash in his bag and told her to help herself.

Her eyes had lit up. *Jesus fucking Christ,* and her intake of breath was a slow whistle of amazement. It had been a while since she had seen anything as good as that.

Later, when Silas thought of Thai, it was her skinny brown arms that he saw, her silver bracelets, the dolphin tattoo on her shoulder blade, and the torn dirty dresses she always wore; that was what he remembered, that and the sharp blue of her eyes as they narrowed with each inhalation of dope, until eventually she just sat there, lids heavy, oblivious to the kids' screams as they knocked over each other's towers, tore each other's drawings, broke each other's toys.

When Silas told her about the house, and his plans for fixing it up, she said she'd wondered why he spent so much time walking around that place.

So, when are you going to start? she asked.

He drew back on the joint. *Don't know,* and he grinned because suddenly it all seemed too much; it was far easier to just sit and imagine what it could be.

No date, hey?

He tapped his feet on the rotten verandah and looked out towards the gulf, amazed for a moment at the sense of peace this amount of dope seemed to be giving him. *Guess not,* he grinned again and they both started laughing. One of her boys was standing opposite with his hands on his hips as he imitated their laugh with his own, *ha ha ha.* The other kids soon followed suit, until they were all around him, the fakeness of their laughter sharp and harsh in the heat, the flies thick on their scabby knees and runny noses.

Piss off, and Thai waved her hand at them as you would wave at insects; pointless putting too much energy into getting rid of them when they would be more than likely to return.

Thai told Silas that she and Matt had been in the town for four years. It was the only place where they could buy not just one house but two. They were going to have a bed and breakfast, they were going to be self-sufficient, they were going to get back to the land; there was a lot they were going to do, problem was she couldn't remember much of it anymore.

Silas told Thai he was going to take photographs, portraits of the residents, or perhaps he would paint, maybe draw, and he would glance up at the great curve of the ranges, the sheer sprawl of them, and wonder how he would capture them.

Yeah? she would say without looking at him, and she would roll another.

Matt was rarely there. He was working on a station, trying to pay off debts. On the occasional nights when he returned, he would sit next to Thai and take the joint she offered him, the youngest girl curling up to sleep in his arms while he smoked in silence. Silas would sit with them and listen to the gentle lap of the tide slipping out, far out, and he would close his eyes, the last of the day's heat still lingering in the early evening, soft and warm.

He once asked Thai who Tricia was and he waved his hand in the direction of the caravan. She stubbed out the end of her joint without looking at him, her bracelets jangling as she ground the tip into the verandah, while Matt got up without a word and went into the house. Silas didn't ask again.

He also asked who Rudi was, but it was not Thai who told him, it was the others: Mick, Jason and Steve. Word of his stash had got around by then, and at night they would pull up in Steve's car, Mick in the back, Jason in the front, all of them in identical jeans, flannel shirts with the sleeves ripped off, beanies and black sunglasses, ready to get down to the serious business of wasting themselves.

Steve had come first, without the others, the low throb of the engine dying to a splutter, the dust settling as he slammed the door and raised a hand in greeting.

Gidday, and Thai had the paper laid out flat on her lap before he had even crossed the dirt that had once been a flower bed.

He didn't acknowledge Silas, not until he had drawn back, deep and hard, and then he turned in his direction.

Not bad, and his look was one of grudging admiration.

Later, when he brought the others, they would all sit on Thai's verandah, the kids inside, asleep on the lounge-room floor, the black and white television a fuzz of light in the darkness of the house. In the soft purple dusk, Silas would tell them what an amazing place this was. *Look at it,* and he would raise his arm in the general direction of the jetty. Stoned and effusive, with the heat of the day gone and the slow drowsiness of the evening's smoke thick in his blood, he was in love with it all.

Mick was the only one who responded. *Yeah?* He turned away. *Try living here.*

In the quiet that followed his remark, Silas heard a neighbour's flyscreen door creaking as she opened it to call the cat; *Sootie,* her voice quavering, the tap of the spoon against the tin of food a sharp punctuation to the repetition of that one word.

Sootie, they all called out in unison, Steve, Jason and Mick, and Thai just watched and grinned as Steve stroked her arm; *here pussy, pussy,* his voice a whisper now as she pretended to purr.

There were things going on in that town that Silas hadn't even begun to guess at, and he let go of his idle fantasies of curling up next to Thai's wiry brown body. He stood up slowly, his legs heavy and tired from sitting for too long. Perhaps he would just go for a swim, there in the black water, he would float out on the slowness of the tide, alone, and as he contemplated the idea he dangled one foot over the edge of the verandah.

That was when he saw him for the second time; the old man he had noticed on the first night, illuminated for a moment as he walked out along the shore, his gait unsteady.

Where'd he come from? Silas asked.

Steve shrugged his shoulders as he sucked hard on the last of his joint and let the butt drop onto the dirt below. He took the smoke that Thai had ready for him. *You don't want to know him,* and he checked to see that Silas was listening because he wanted to be recognised as the source of knowledge, the one with authority, the protector, even to an outsider. It was clearly a role that deserved respect, and

Silas knew he had to somehow muster a serious look on his face.

Jason knocked over the can at his feet as he attempted to stand and Mick just kept smoking, his eyes fixed on the darkness of the road.

Rudi Weiss, Steve began, lighting the new joint. *Lives out of town. Set up a fuckin' commune with a group of wackos who poisoned local stock as soon as they saw a hoofprint on the place. Said they were killing the country,* and Steve shook his head in amazement, *cattle, killing the country,* and his eyes closed as he let out a thin stream of smoke.

Silas took the joint that Thai held out for him. *What happened?* The dope was sweet and thick in the back of his throat, and as he stared out across the darkness of the yard, he realised he had failed to complete his question. *To the others?*

Steve tilted his head back and took a long swig of beer. *Got tired of living in la la land and left.*

Mick was standing now, looking as though he was making a move to go, but not quite getting it together.

But Rudi stayed, and Steve shook his head again. *Moved out to the tip and planted a fuckin' garden.*

Silas felt the heaviness of the dope flood him and he closed his eyes as he leant back against the verandah post. That was something he wouldn't mind seeing. He would go there, he thought, when he got it together; that's what he would do.

He must have drifted off to sleep. He couldn't remember. But when he woke, they were gone, Thai, Jason, Mick and Steve. He pulled himself up, the roughness of the post scratching his hands, and he stumbled into the lounge room. He had to pick his way over the still bodies of the kids, he had to feel his way in the darkness to where he knew his bed was, somewhere out there, somewhere in that cottage out the back.

— 3 —

It was Valentina and Semyon Kirlian who invented the technique used to photograph the electromagnetic field that surrounds all we can see and touch. The images are like thousands of flares of light, dancing and moving, a galaxy within a galaxy.

The discovery that these photographs could reveal an ailment before it had manifested itself was an accidental one. Holding his hand up before the camera, Semyon found he could not get the usual pattern of emanations to appear. It was not a fault in the equipment; he checked and rechecked it, each time finding that there was nothing wrong. The problem was an illness, a change that was already there in his body, although it had not yet revealed itself. That was what caused the alteration to the image, a sickness that was not to strike him until some time after he took the photograph.

This was how Constance saw the world, or at least that was what Rudi had told Silas.

Not the object itself, but the force that surrounds it. That is what she sees.

Silas would look at his own hand, wanting to see what lay beyond the flesh in front of him. If Rudi had spoken the truth, Constance may have seen the changes in him before the ailments from which he now suffered had begun to manifest themselves. With his palms open on the desk in front of him, Silas wanted to know when the change had occurred, when the rot had begun; was it after he met her, or had he gone to her with it all set in place, there inside him before he even laid eyes on her?

With his fingers pressed tight against his eyelids, he still saw her. He always saw her. Constance, there in that garden, next to the peppercorn tree.

— *4* —

We all have selected intimacies we like to reveal, but they are usually far less personal than they appear. They have been used often, they have been shaped and worn, and that is why we choose them. They are intended to reveal our own fragility, to draw another in, but they usually reveal very little at all.

Greta was, and may still be, less careful than most of us in what she will tell. She wants to truly show herself, hoping that this inner core will be accepted, her wide blue eyes bright as she opens herself up yet again, regretting what she has said soon after she has said it. This is how I remember her, and in some ways, when I met up with her again, it seemed that little had changed. She told me everything about her and Silas, but perhaps these revelations were simply a product of nervousness. She was, at first, skittish, pulling back from the prospect of talking about us, telling me about him instead because he was, after all, the only thing we now had in common (except, of course, the discomfort we each felt about our past).

However, when it came to discussing the details of the time she spent with me in her conversations with Silas, I know that she was, at first, somewhat more circumspect about what she revealed. From what I could gather, it seems she initially said very little. As they walked home together, Silas began to open up to her, not about Port Tremaine (he, too, was cautious in the revelations he chose), but about his father's demise in the business world, the extent of his wrongdoings, and about his own inability to deal with it.

I have always just thrown my hands up, pretending that there's nothing I can do, he admitted, ashamed at his ineffectualness. *It seemed too hard. I don't know how to even begin to right some of the wrongs.*

She listened to him, and he, in turn, listened to her, as she told him about her mother's death when she was five years old. Her father could not cope, she said. He left her with her mother's parents and returned to Sweden, remarrying within a couple of years.

And you never see him? Silas asked.

She shook her head.

Greta told Silas she had always been in trouble. By the time she was fifteen she had run away five times, once hitchhiking interstate, another time stealing a neighbour's car. She slept with other girls' boyfriends, even the local librarian's husband, and once the maths teacher at high school.

Silas smiled. *Not the best way to behave in a small country town.*

She didn't argue.

I was a mess, she admitted. *I probably still am.*

One evening, as they both watched an ibis pick its way delicately across the darkening parklands, she attempted to ask Silas what I was like now, hesitant about touching on the subject, but curious all the same.

When Silas asked her if we had been together for long, she told him that our relationship was fairly brief.

But it took me a while to recover.

In telling him her stories, Greta probably wanted to let Silas know that her distance with him was not just due to the strangeness of his behaviour. She was no good at relationships, she would have tried to explain, wanting to take some of the blame for the nervousness they both felt in each other's company, wanting, rightly or wrongly, to make him feel better. She liked Silas, more so as they spent time together, and she wanted to rewrite what had happened between them. She wanted to recast the story, to wipe away how troubled he was. *She* was a mess and that was why she was being careful. Unfortunately, it was not so easy to forget the way in which she had found him, sitting in the darkness of the kitchen, his complete absorption in inflicting pain upon himself both terrifying and confusing, and with each step that she took towards him, there would always be another one back.

Reaching the park gate some weeks after the night they slept together, the first of the evening lights flickering across the harbour, she searched for her phone in her bag. She had to go. Normally, they would have walked up the twisting hill that leads past the docks, parting on the corner of his street, but tonight she was meeting a friend. She was about to tell Silas she would see him next week, when he reached for her, awkwardly, and asked her if she wanted to have a meal with him.

I know it's Friday night, and you've probably had something organised for months, but you just look so beautiful in this light, and he grinned shyly at her.

Don't, and she wished her surprise had not given a harshness to her voice that had not been intended, because even though she had been wanting this interest, she found herself floundering in the face of it.

She could see that Silas felt like a fool, and she tried to apologise. Maybe they could go out next week, she suggested, and when they parted, she kissed him, clumsily, on the cheek.

As she walked up the road that leads past the art gallery and into the city, Silas watched her disappear into the darkness. There was a softness around her, a lilac haze, and for one brief moment it seemed to him she was a part of the deep purple of the evening sky.

He hailed a taxi, wishing he had said nothing, and as he

remembered the look on her face he could feel it beginning, the tightening that started in his heart and pulled in along his entire left side. He winced as he gave his address and closed his eyes in preparation for the onslaught of pain.

Are you all right? The driver looked into the rear-vision mirror as he pulled away from the kerb.

Silas nodded. It was all he was capable of doing.

s p i d e r

Tarentula

Clinical. – – Angina pectoris . . .

Characteristics. – – . . . Nunez is our chief authority. He instigated the proving and collected much outside information on the action of the poison. 'Tarantella' is a dance named from the city of Tarentum. 'Tarantism' is a dancing mania, set up in persons bitten by the *Tarentula*, or in those who imagine themselves bitten. The cure is music and dancing . . . Francis Mustel, a peasant, was bitten by a tarentula on the left hand, about the middle of July, as he was gathering corn. He went home with his companions but on the way fell as if struck by apoplexy. Dyspnoea followed, and face, hands, and feet became dark. Knowing the remedy, his companions fetched musicians. When the patient heard their playing he began to revive, to sigh, to move first his feet, then his hands, and then the whole body; at last getting on his feet he took to dancing violently, with sighing so laboured that the bystanders were almost frightened . . . Two hours after the music began the blackness of his face and hands went off, he sweated freely, and regained perfect health.

John Henry Clarke MD, *A Dictionary of Practical Materia Medica*

— *1* —

Silas told me that it took about three weeks for his dope supply to run out. He couldn't be certain, in fact he had no firm idea of how long he spent wasting his days on Thai's verandah, but that was his guess.

It was Thai who first noticed, reaching into the bag, only to find it empty. The plants she and Matt had grown had long since died, but she was sure Steve could fix them up. He knew someone in the town on the other side of the gulf. The problem was the money, and her eyes had narrowed as she had looked at him.

Silas had just nodded, but when he saw her reach for the phone, he knew she thought he'd agreed to pay. He opened his mouth to speak, and then decided against it. He didn't have the energy to argue with her.

Stepping out into the hard glare of the morning, he saw the dirt choking the yard, the ruin that had once been his mother's place, the pot-holed road, the few desert oaks hanging limp in the heat, and beyond all that the undulating roll of those ranges, baking under the unrelenting sun. His mouth was dry and his skin clammy as he surveyed the scene, not wanting to see what was undeniably there in front of his eyes.

The night before, as he had attempted to stretch out on his single bed, he had let his mind float, luxuriating in images of how wild and inhospitable this country was, how empty, how unaccommodating to even the most basic of human needs. With his neck against the iron bedstead and his feet hanging over the edge, he had been amazed at the change he had made in his life. He was here and he liked it. He would start on the house soon, and as his thoughts had rolled lazily across the possibilities, he had heard the huski-ness of Thai's laughter as Steve had slammed the bedroom door shut, the whole house shuddering for a moment, and the peace in which he had immersed himself had vanished as quickly as it had appeared. Wanting only to sleep, he had found himself remembering one of his last conversations with his mother. They had talked as they had always talked, Silas knowing she was half listening, the alcohol blurring all he said so that his words had simply formed a pleasant cloud to be shaped as she pleased. It was only when he had been about to hang up that he had asked her, uncertain as to why the question had suddenly come to his mind, whether he had been a difficult child.

She had been silent for a moment. When she had finally spoken, her voice had been small.

I loved you.

I know, he had said.

It was a hard time.

Lying on the bed out the back of Thai's, Silas had recalled the peripatetic nature of their lives and how, through it all, his mother had never thought to leave his father. Even when she was hopelessly drunk, her misery at their homelessness palpable beneath the taut surface of her inebriated joy, there was a softness in her gaze, a visible easing in her tension whenever his father had entered the room, whenever he had looked at her with adoration in his eyes, always completely unaware of the wrongs he had committed, always choosing to believe that one day he would be vindicated, that his version of events would be believed. She had loved him. She had seen him for what he was and she had not stopped loving him.

As he had tried to sleep, Silas had felt his aloneness, and he had wanted, more than anything, the warmth of another body beside him, someone to affirm his existence in the strangeness of this place. He had closed his eyes, only to start, visibly jerking as he had felt his body falling, and there was pure panic as he had wondered why he had come here and what he had to go back to.

Now, in the morning, the dryness of the heat was harsh on his back and shoulders and the emptiness crushed him. He glanced briefly at the ruin of the house next door and then closed his eyes. For a moment, the possibility of going over there and lying down in the midst of its collapse crossed his mind. He would clear a small space in the rubble and filth and curl up. He shook his head and swiped, yet again, at the flies, his entire body agitated by the stillness at which he had once again arrived.

Thai's kids were stacking old tyres in a heap, forming a tower next to a pile of rubbish at the side of the house. The oldest boy, who was about nine, was ordering his younger brother to bring the next one over. Silas watched the boy sweating, every muscle in his skinny body strained as he tried to carry it to the indicated spot. He had never noticed until now that the older one didn't talk. Each of his instructions to his brother, who was clearly the slave in this architectural feat, was mimed with a strange mixture of hand signals and urgent mouthing.

He was bitten by a dingo, the younger one explained. A lizard flicked through the dirt and he bent down to grab it, quick and sure, the tail coming off in his hands. He held it up proudly, a worm twitching between his fingers. *Hurts him to open his mouth. It's his jaw,* and the older brother tilted his head up to show Silas the long jagged scar that cut around the base of his chin.

Really? Silas asked.

Really, and they both nodded solemnly.

Silas glanced at the tyres stacked next to the piles of

garbage and, without thinking, told them he wanted to go to the garden, the one in the rubbish dump. The sudden realisation that this was what he would do filled him with an overpowering sense of relief, the strength of the sensation almost making him nauseous as he reeled back from the possibility of the fall that had been dogging him all morning.

The younger boy pointed one skinny arm towards the right of the jetty, the lizard's tail still dangling between his fingers. *It's that way,* and he sniffed, the snot disappearing up his nostril, only to run down again, thick and yellow, moments later.

The older one shook his head furiously and started scratching a drawing in the dirt, the chickens pecking at the edges of the marks he made.

He's drawing you a map. He says it's past two stone places and then there's a tree.

No. The older boy stamped his feet angrily, kicking up a cloud of dust, the hens scattering and squawking.

The sudden loudness of his voice shocked Silas. Rubbing at the grit in his eyes, now mingled with a slow trickle of sweat from his forehead, he looked at the two of them.

He can talk when he wants to, the younger one explained. *It's just that it hurts,* and he attempted to grasp Silas's arm as he turned to walk away. *It's true,* he protested.

As Silas swung each leg over what remained of the gate,

as he tried to shoo the chickens back inside, he could still hear the younger boy: *Don't you want to know how to get there? To the garden?*

He just shook his head and walked on.

– 2 –

Tarentula. It was not a difficult choice for a first remedy. It had, in fact, sprung to my mind when I first saw Silas, and I had to be careful that the questions I asked did not simply guide me to the conclusion I had already formed. I had to keep an open mind, while not ignoring that immediate hunch.

This is the way it sometimes is with patients. When I first treated Larissa (one of my provers), she immediately struck me as a person who would benefit from Aurum. From the moment I saw her in the waiting room, sitting in a shaft of sunlight, I had a sense. There was something in the dullness of her eyes, the heaviness of her expression, and as she began to tell me of her depression, that she had no heart for anything, that the light had gone from her life, I knew that I had been right.

It is not always like that (rarely, actually), and I have found that it usually occurs when I have some kind of affinity with the patient. After Larissa left, I realised there was a sadness in her smile that had reminded me of my mother

and that even some of the phrases she'd used had been identical to the way in which my mother would try to describe
how she felt when she had a breakdown, wanting me to
understand that it was nothing I had done, her tone insistent
each time she saw the doubt in my eyes.

In Silas's case, this affinity was less tangible but perhaps
closer to home. The extreme change in his life, the extent
of the isolation he had now chosen disturbed me. At the
end of our sessions together, I would sometimes catch
myself staring out the window, my own reflection looking
back at me, and I would wonder at what I had become
and why.

Silas did not ask me what the remedy was when I gave it
to him. He just glanced briefly at the instructions I had written out for him, seven drops, morning, noon and night for
three days, and made another appointment.

The next time I saw him he wanted to know more. He
was not interested in what it was he had been taking (he had
read the label on the bottle), he wanted to know how it
worked. That session, if I remember correctly, was also the
first time he spoke of Constance.

So, how are things? I asked, sensing his agitation from the
moment he sat down.

He told me the pains were a little less acute and not as
frequent.

But still there?

He nodded. He was holding the remedy in his hand, rolling it back and forth. The click of the bottle against the table was louder than he had intended as he put it down between us.

If this is what you say it is, then surely it's poisonous? He pointed to the label and looked directly at me.

It's been diluted to such an extent that it has no toxic effects.

Silas raised his eyebrows. *Then how can it work?*

I picked the remedy up and then put it down again. Silas's question did not come as a surprise. It is not uncommon for patients to ask me how it is possible, thinking that I am going to reveal a magic trick to them. As I attempt to give some form of understandable explanation, their eyes usually glaze over; it is not magic after all.

We are all trained to see the world in a particular way, and Silas did not take his gaze from mine as I told him I needed him to think a little differently, to throw away notions he held as truths.

The more diluted a substance is, and I held up the bottle, *the more powerful it is.*

His stare remained fixed.

And what is poison to some is antidote to others.

He told me he had never liked riddles.

I apologised. I had not intended to be obtuse and I sat back for a moment as I tried to assess the best way in which to give him an understanding of what we were attempting to achieve. I asked him to think of the body as a vibrating field, *more complex than you can imagine.*

I realise now that Silas would have been reminded of the words Rudi had uttered, each time he had tried to describe Constance's vision.

Everything has an electromagnetic force, a particular frequency at which it resonates.

Silas would have remembered the heat, the stillness of Rudi's shack and the intensity of Rudi's gaze.

I continued: *When you are sick, when something has affected your body – love, loss, a bacteria, heat, anything – to such an extent that the vibrational plane alters significantly, your body will react in the best way it can to restore its balance. It produces a defence mechanism, and this may manifest itself with stomach cramps, heart pains, perhaps nightmares.*

Silas was trying to understand.

In simple terms, what I want is to find a substance that resonates at the same frequency as this defence mechanism. I want to boost the strength of the body's attempts to counter what has gone wrong. The defence mechanism vibrates with a greater force when it is stimulated by a wave of similar frequency. I am trying to help the body to heal itself.

Silas picked up the remedy and looked at the neatly typed label.

This particular venom would produce certain symptoms in a 'well' person, very similar to the symptoms you suffer, because it has the same frequency, and I paused, hoping he had understood. *And the more diluted it is, the greater force it will have. Actually, it has been diluted so much that there is none of the original matter left. What remains is the energy. Just the energy.*

In the cool calm of the clinic, Silas picked at a loose thread on his jumper. *Have you heard of anyone actually being able to see this vibrating force?*

I looked at him a little curiously. *There are photographs.*

Silas could tell I did not know what he had meant. *I know,* he said, impatiently, *but have you ever heard of anyone actually being able to see it?*

I considered the question for a moment. *There are healers, aura readers. Some are genuine and some I wouldn't trust,* and I nodded my head in the direction of the front door, to where the corridor branched out to the other rooms in the building, raising my eyebrows as I did so.

I met someone. Silas faltered.

When?

When I was there, in that place.

I glanced across at the computer screen, running my eyes down his notes. *Port Tremaine?*

Silas nodded. He could see that I was weighing up whether to continue with the conversation or whether to direct it to a close. I was trying to assess the situation quickly, to ascertain whether we were about to delve into the roots of the matter or take a sidetrack that would only waste time for both of us.

Silas knew this, but he could not bring himself to help in making the decision. He did not know if he wanted to embark on the subject that was opening in front of us.

Do I continue with this? he held up the bottle, attempting to change the topic.

I scrolled down the screen to the end of the last session's notes and then turned, slowly, towards him. *Tell me,* I said, *a little more about this person.*

Silas looked out the window. *Constance.*

I waited.

She died. He closed his eyes, rubbing his thumb gently across his forefinger, the pressure gradually increasing. *Snake bite.* He breathed in sharply. *I couldn't save her. It took too long to get help.*

He was silent. When he turned to look at me, his gaze was cool, remote. He looked back at the window, and I thought for a moment that he was not going to speak again, that I would need to ask another question, but then he opened his mouth, and his words were soft in the quiet.

I loved her.

I leant a little closer.

At least, that was what I told myself. He closed his eyes again, his voice so faint now I could barely hear it. *That is the excuse I have tried to use.*

— 3 —

Port Tremaine is surrounded by desert country, great tracts
so parched that even the saltbush struggles to grow in the
sandy soil. It is country that sweeps in golden arcs towards
the red ranges sprawling under a harsh blue sky, burning
dust in the summer, freezing dirt in the winter. It is country
that is coarse and bare, with the little vegetation that man-
ages to survive sticking up like mangy tufts of hair on a hide
that had long since been rubbed back to a worn leather.

Silas sat on the sand and looked in amazement at the
world lying beyond the cyclone fencing. It was, he told me,
jewel-encrusted. It was, he said, surreal.

China blues, shimmering scarlets, bitter yellows, crim-
sons that throbbed against forest greens, ivory creams that
twisted silken against soft pinks; Silas told me that he stared
like someone who had been starved of colour, who wanted
to gather it all into his arms, heap it and crush it and bury
his face in it, and as he pressed his nose up against the pad-
locked gate and looked at the twists and turns of the paths
that led through the garden to the shack in the centre, each

one thick with flowers, he wondered what it was that he had discovered.

Unnatural, Pearl had told him when he had gone to her after leaving Thai's hoping she would direct him to Rudi's. He had held onto that one word from the moment she had uttered it, wanting a story, a tale to lift him out of the state into which he had been descending.

Sitting in the darkest corner of her shop, crocheting one of her rugs that never sold, Pearl had not looked up as the door had swung shut behind him; she had not glanced in his direction until he had finished recounting the boys' attempts to describe the quickest way out to the garden.

It sounds unbelievable, he had said, wanting to encourage her to create with him a picture of whatever it was he was hoping to find.

He had watched her select the next colour for her design, holding up balls of wool against the pattern, and he had wondered for a moment whether he might faint. Despite the fact that the sun did not penetrate beneath the tattered canvas awning that hung across the street, the lack of air in the room made it almost unbearable. He could see the damp sweat under her arms, staining the floral print of her frock, and the loose folds of her flesh, waving slightly, as she clicked the crochet hook in and out of a purple wool.

Visitors aren't welcome, and she had leant forward to make sure Silas was listening. *He takes a gun to people who sniff around.*

Silas had pulled back. *Why?*

A fly had buzzed near her head and she had reached for a rolled up newspaper to swat it with. The slam had slapped through the stillness.

When's the repairs starting? and she had nodded in the direction of his mother's house.

Soon, he had told her, knowing that any attempt to lead her back to the story would only fail, and he had watched in fascination as she stood up, her weight forcing her to take it step by careful step, the squashed fly balanced on the edge of the newspaper, constantly threatening to topple off as she had lumbered, heavily, towards the bin.

Suppose you've been organising the builders for the past few weeks, and she had snorted as she sat down again.

Silas hadn't bothered to correct her.

You know he has a daughter?

He had leant forward, his smile wide and cheeky. *Locked up?*

Pearl had winked at him. *Beautiful as the morning and blind as the night. She's the one that grows everything. Poisons, the lot of them. Wouldn't let your dog go up there, if you had one that is. Doubt whether he'd come back alive.*

He had assured her he would be careful and he had been surprised, for a moment, at the flicker of fear he'd felt, tinged with a new excitement, sharp and quick in his blood.

Sitting outside that cyclone fencing, mesmerised by the spectacular vision in front of him, Silas found the one thought that kept returning to him was the word Pearl had used: *unnatural.* A strange description for a place that could not have been more abundant with nature.

He was, conceivably, still ripped. He was, perhaps, still far from himself, still as gone as he had been each night on that verandah with Thai, because what he saw here was, quite simply, impossible. He did not understand how it could exist and yet there it was, right in front of him, and he pulled himself up, leaning his entire body into the fencing.

Hello, he called out, not seeing her, not immediately. *Hello.*

She was standing right there, only fifty metres away, and staring at him. He forgot that Pearl had told him she was blind, her gaze seemed so focused on him, and as he raised his hand to signal a greeting, she stepped forward: Constance, tall, poised and more exquisite than any of the flowers that clustered around her.

I wouldn't come any closer, she warned, and she nodded in the direction of the shack, back towards Rudi, who was making his way down the path towards Silas, a gun in his hand.

— 4 —

I know there is a small part of me that wanted to see what Silas saw. When I drove to Port Tremaine, I went to find out whether he had returned, but this was not the only reason for my detour. I wanted some truth to the vision he had attempted to describe for me, I too wanted to see it, extraordinary and beautiful, spread out in front of me.

Was I delusional? Silas once asked me, and then he stared out the window, aware that I was unable to answer his question. *I had smoked so much dope, I was such a mess,* he searched for a reason and then lapsed into silence.

He did not know. He would never know.

Greta did not go to the library on the weekends, and nor did Silas, usually, but on the Saturday morning after he first spoke to me about the garden he was there, without the distraction of her in front of him.

The reading room was almost empty and he took a seat, the scrape of the chair loud in the silence. He found a blank piece of paper and laid it on the desk, determined that this time he would get somewhere.

Dear Rudi

He wished there were a better way of beginning.

I need to tell you what happened, but each time I attempt to I am overwhelmed by how impossible it now all seems.

p e a r l

Calcarea Carbonica. – – . . . a trituration of the middle layer of oyster shells.

John Henry Clarke, *A Dictionary of Practical Materia Medica*

Of the whole [mollusc] family, the oyster has the most undifferentiated body and possesses no limbs whatsoever. The animal is completely encased in its shell and absolutely immobile, since it is attached to a rock. Its only visible life expression consists in the slight opening and closing of the shell . . . *Calcarea* is standstill, passivity, immobility, clinging, restraining, peripherally enclosing, restricting, ingoing, the negative or holding-in receptive principle.

Edward C Whitmont, *Psyche and Substance: Essays on Homeopathy in the Light of Jungian Psychology*

— *1* —

When Silas returned from Port Tremaine, the few friends he ran into would occasionally ask him what he had been doing while he was there.

Nothing much, he usually said, not once making mention of Constance, her father, or the garden in which they lived.

As the weeks passed and the change that had occurred in him became inescapably obvious to everyone who had known him, Silas was no longer faced with the possibility of having to discuss the time he had spent away, and he was relieved. It was not until he saw Jake, about eight months after he had come home, that the topic inevitably came up, once again.

Jake had also been out of the city.

India, he told Silas. *Studying Ashtanga.*

Jake was the first person to ask him whether he had fallen in love. He had followed Silas into his apartment building but when they reached the lift, Silas had told him he was only going up for a few moments, he had to go out. Even though the relief that sex might bring was tempting, it was never really a possibility. The aversion he had developed to any kind of closeness was too strong, and, unable to express this, he had simply made up an excuse.

Did anything happen to you out there? Jake looked at Silas curiously. He had always prided himself on his ability to read people, he said he could see the *energy flow*, a phrase that Silas found as irritating as Jake's tendency to do the splits at every given opportunity.

Did you fall in love? Jake asked.

Silas shook his head. *No,* he assured him, his response emphatic.

Greta also asked him the same question when he first spoke of Port Tremaine to her. It was on the night they slept together, when they were out drinking, that Silas told her he had not always been a recluse. He had changed, he said, after that trip. In the haze of the alcohol, he thought for a moment that he had mentioned Port Tremaine to her previously.

What trip? she asked him, and he gave her only the barest details.

What happened? She grinned. *Did you fall in love?*

His response was similar to the one he had given Jake.

Out there? He laughed. *God, no,* and he butted out his cigarette with short sharp jabs, even though he had lit it only moments before.

When he told me that he had been in love with Constance, I could see that he was surprised by his own words, and that he was immediately aware of how ambiguous the truth of that statement was.

For many of us, the mention of love brings with it a myriad of qualifications; we use the word and then we start trying to hedge it in, to shape it, to give it some kind of definition.

This morning, walking with Larissa as the sun was burning the frost off the short grass that covers the plains, she told me that she and her partner had decided to marry. I was pleased for her. I know the difficulties they have had, and I know they have worked hard to resolve them.

In the distance, a group of kangaroos watched us. Pausing in their grazing to assess whether we presented a threat, they sat up on their hind legs, all eyes on us as we made our way towards an outcrop of boulders on the highest point.

She asked me if I was in a relationship, if I was in love with anyone.

Not at the moment, I told her.

It has, in fact, been just over a year and a half since Victoria left. She is pregnant now, an issue that was a cause of considerable contention between us, and she is, I believe, happy.

I have not met anyone since we separated. I have not even slept with anyone, and I shake my head as I realise this.

Any reason? Larissa asked and she glanced across at me, averting her eyes almost immediately.

I smiled at her. *There isn't one in particular that I can pin-point. It just doesn't interest me much.*

She apologised for asking. *I shouldn't have. It's only because we are here in this place. You know, not in the clinic.*

I told her it was fine, that I didn't mind at all.

Look. It was the kangaroos that I was indicating to her and I watched as they bounded away, arcs of white frost shimmering behind them with each enormous leap they made.

It was only when they were gone that I realised her eyes had in fact remained on me, and in that brief moment before she turned away, I was surprised to see that her look was one of mild curiosity, almost sympathy, as though I was a being she could not fathom.

— 2 —

Silas told me that it took him five minutes to convince Rudi to unlock the gate. One look at Constance had been enough for him to know he wanted to go in. She was, he said, more beautiful than he would have believed to be possible. Her hair was thick and dark and it fell, black and smooth, to her shoulder blades. Her skin, and he searched for the words, was like the palest petal, touched pink and stretched taut across the fingers. But it was her eyes that stilled him: they were violet, deep and pure, the colour of the dusk after a perfect summer day. Standing just outside that gate, his floundering heart wide open to it all, Silas wanted only to be on the other side, there with her.

He had not, of course, heard of Rudi's work; he had no knowledge of the recognition he had once achieved, albeit obscure. It was, therefore, simply a matter of luck that he chose to tell Rudi he was interested in writing an article about the garden, the lie he had stumbled upon working almost immediately.

When he saw the old man's grip on the gun loosen

slightly, the blood return to his knuckles and the muscles in his arms relax, Silas pressed on, telling him he had heard of the community Rudi had set up, that he wanted to know more, that he would not take too much of his time.

You are in the same field? Rudi asked.

Silas saw him reach for his keys. *I am interested in plants.*

It is not just plants we use. Rudi was at the gate now, fumbling with the lock. *It is anything and everything. That is the wonder of it.*

Silas agreed eagerly, knowing that Constance was listening, her eyes on him, not seeing him, but assessing him, judging him. He turned to her, the gate clanging shut behind him.

You've grown all this? he asked, taking one step closer to her and then, stunned by a rich sweet perfume that seemed to cling to her, he pulled back.

Somehow she was aware that it was her, and not her father, he had been addressing and she smiled, amused. *They are the ones that do the growing.* Her eyes held his.

I had heard how extraordinary this place was, his words came out in a rush as he attempted to keep her attention, *but I never expected anything like this.*

Her smile vanished as quickly as it had appeared, and it was Rudi who spoke. *You have read my articles?*

Silas could not take his eyes from Constance as he lied. *Some.*

And you write for?

Different publications. He was aware that Constance was still facing him, and he remembered, with some relief, that she would not be able to see the rush of crimson across his cheeks.

He turned to her; *I have never seen you in town.*

I don't go there. Her tone was dismissive, and then she touched her father's arm gently as she said that she would leave them to talk.

Come, Rudi beckoned.

The path that led to the shack was shaded by trees. The light fell in dancing pools at Silas's feet as he followed, reluctantly. He had never seen such a place: the gentle sway of the branches against the clear blue sky, the soft rustle of the leaves, the sweetness of the flowers that clung to him as he passed, the damp velvet of their petals smooth against his skin; it was intoxicating.

Everything I built myself, Rudi told him proudly. *Everything I found, nothing was bought. This stove,* and he pointed to an old Kooka that took up most of the kitchen annex, *just thrown out.*

Imbeciles, and he waved his hand impatiently to indicate the outside world. *New, new, new, that is all they want. They are killing this land with their greed for new. It is dying on them. But do they listen? Pah,* and he shrugged his shoulders in exasperation.

Through the window, Silas could see her. She was adjusting a temporary shade rigged over one of the garden beds, long tassels of brilliant pink flowers falling around her (*love-lies-bleeding*, she was to tell him later), pausing for a moment to feel the direction of the sun before turning back to the task.

This, and Rudi pointed to the garden, *shows what can be done. When we came here, after the others left, it was all sick, diseased, but now it grows.*

As Silas stepped away from the window, he noticed that smell once again, the fullness of the perfume that had clung to Constance also pervading the closeness of the shack. He looked for flowers, but there were none.

There was only one room, two single beds, a table and two chairs, but despite the lack of furniture, the place was cluttered. There were books everywhere, Silas had never seen so many: piled high on the stove, the floor, stacked into the few shelves that had been rigged along the walls, they filled the place.

We will talk, and Rudi pulled out the chair, clearing a small space at the table for him.

Has she always been blind? Silas turned back to where Constance worked, the pale blue of her shirt shining soft against the brilliance of the day.

She sees. More than you or I will ever see.

Unaware that they were watching her, she stood, slowly stretching herself in the shade, her face turned up towards the clear arc of the sky, and Silas was certain he could see her smile.

She has the art. Rudi wrapped his fingers around Silas's arm. *All of my knowledge I have given to her. But she has more than that.* He looked out to her, his eyes softening as he watched her bend back towards her work.

Silas could feel the pressure of Rudi's fingers on his skin, and he knew that when he turned he would see the eagerness on Rudi's face. It was clear that this was something he had wanted, for who knows how long; a chance to talk, to be understood, to be recognised.

Where shall we begin?

Silas had not even opened his mouth to respond before Rudi continued, waving his hand dismissively, as he answered his own question: *I am not interested in the past. It is not worthy of discussion. What happened to the others happened. They did not have the dedication, the patience, the perseverance, and so they left.*

Silas nodded.

It is our work now that matters, the progress we are making, and as Rudi gathered his papers, Silas turned once again, shifting his chair a little so that he could steal a glance at her each time Rudi's attention was diverted, because it would, he feared, be a long afternoon; unbearable if it weren't for the sight of her, right there, just outside the window.

— 3 —

It is difficult for me to remember the initial attraction I had
for Greta – everything became overshadowed by her desperate need – but I can't (and shouldn't) completely deny
the fact that it did once exist.

She was, and is, beautiful. Tall and pale with wide nervous eyes and long slender hands that move rapidly when she
talks. She always drank too much, smoked too much and she
was always intense. She was a year below me at college and,
even though I did not know her, I had noticed her. We all
had. We had witnessed her fights with boyfriends who
dropped her off and picked her up, her tears in the cafeteria,
her inability to sit still for long, her passions for particular
causes that would wane only moments later; she was a
presence that you felt.

Sometimes I saw her out and we would grin at each
other across a crowded bar, acknowledging each other and
the fact that we were, unlike so many of the other students, clinging to our vices. I was often with someone, and
so was she, but regardless of that, I would not have gone

out of my way to get to know her, I would not have pursued her.

Yet when we did start spending time together, it was, to my surprise, far more enjoyable than I would have expected. I discovered that a one-on-one conversation with her was disarmingly alive. She loved to sit up and talk, and not only did she want to talk, she wanted to draw out revelations from the person she was with. I remember the empathy in her eyes, the way in which she leant forward and asked questions, wanting to know more, and how it was, at first, enormously seductive.

So I can understand why Silas felt connected to her, why she was the first person to whom he attempted to speak about the wounds he was inflicting upon himself. It was not just that she had seen him in the act, it was also that he felt he could trust her, he felt she would listen.

When he woke, the clock on the mantelpiece clicked over. It was four in the morning and, although it was cold, Silas could feel the sweat down his back and the fire in his throat. He did not move. At the foot of his bed, a spider was spinning a web across the corner of the room. It was illuminated by the street light and Silas could see each thread, still sticky, and the intricacy of the pattern in its making, the pause before the drop, the swing to the next point, the pause.

He stood up slowly, his limbs aching and exhausted. Even

in the dark, he could make out the sharp gouges in his arms. He turned away when he passed the mirror in the hall, not wanting to face what he had become.

When he began to talk to me, he told me that the first time it happened was shortly after his return from Port Tremaine. He had woken to find the man he had brought home staring at him in terror.

What the fuck are you doing to yourself? The look on his face had been one of complete repulsion.

Somehow, he had come to be sitting on the floor in the kitchen, the tiles cold beneath his skin, his arms covered in blood.

Silas had watched as the man had gathered his clothes from the bedroom floor, never once taking his eyes off him as he had backed towards the door, dressing himself as fast as he could, and letting himself out. Silas had heard him pressing the elevator button over and over again, agitated, wanting it to arrive, the door finally clanging shut behind him, loud in the quiet of the night.

He had looked down at his own flesh. They were holes he had cut, deep holes that he had carved out with a knife, and he had stared at them in disbelief.

When he slept with Greta, it had been a couple of years since anyone had stayed the night. Drunk and attracted to her, he had decided to take the risk.

The next morning, when she had told him how she had

found him, how she had tried to stop him, he had flinched, knowing how likely it was that he would have attempted to hurt her had she got in his way.

I couldn't hold you still, and she had turned to the window in order to avoid his gaze.

She had not shown Silas the bruises on her own arms, but he had seen them, her pale skin purpling in the early morning light.

You thrashed and you shouted, and Greta had kept her eyes fixed on a branch of the tree that grew outside his kitchen. *And then,* she had paused for a moment, *it was like you blacked out.*

Silas did not tell her this was a relief that came too rarely. More often than not he would wake, and that was how he would stay, eyes wide open until the first colouring of the sky, the first tentative birdsong. It was only then that he would allow himself to relax, his entire body tight from the pain; he would finally lie back, exhausted, too tired to sleep despite his relief at the night having passed.

He needed to talk to someone. He needed help, and as he lay in bed that morning, it was Greta he thought of, it was Greta he wanted to see.

— *4* —

Once he had begun to speak of Constance to me, Silas did not stop.

She was, he said, worthy of the words Pearl had used, *as beautiful as the morning*. But this was not, by itself, the reason why he had kept going back there.

There was more to it than that, he told me, trying to explain what it was that had attracted him.

Here again? she would say on the few occasions she happened to be near the gate when Rudi came to let him in, and she would smile, just slightly, as she turned to face him.

It was this elusiveness and the whole fairytale nature of her existence that enticed him. The little he knew about her, the lack of contact he had with her, the way in which she always seemed to appear when he had just about given up on any hope of seeing her, and the way in which she would disappear, slipping back into the lushness of the garden; all of it fascinated him.

Thai was no help. She was not, Silas told me, particularly

fond of conversation, and she was at her least talkative when she was on the other side of a dope-smoking binge such as the one they had all indulged in during his first few weeks in the town.

She did not want to hear Silas's enthusiastic descriptions of the garden, nor did she display any inclination towards answering the numerous questions he had about Constance each night he returned, frustrated that he had once again been unable to talk to her alone, that she had been there, but just out of reach, always just out of reach. Thai would slap the meals on the table, an alternating diet of tinned spaghetti and Vegemite sandwiches, her eyes small and mean as she called the kids in, their names all running into one long, unpronounceable word: *Elilucasjadesass.*

She was waiting for word from Steve. She did not say this, but Silas knew. Each time they heard his car, the deep menace of that engine often the only sound in the night, she would tense slightly, her thin shoulders hunched forward as she drew back on the cigarette, listening; was he coming this way?

Silas did not care. He was swimming in visions of Constance, floating in the new-found knowledge of her existence, and all else had ceased to matter. The desolation of the town, the ruin of his mother's house and his failure to do anything about it, even the fact that Thai had been ripped off, or, more to the point, he had been ripped off (it was his money, after all); it was all of little importance to him.

No deal yet, Steve kept telling them. *Won't be long but.*

As he walked home in the late afternoon, the ranges darkening behind him, Silas would plot ways of being alone with Constance. Crossing the last of the sand and scrub that borders the dusty grid of streets, thinking only of her, he would see Steve parked out on the edge of the dirt track with Shelley sitting next to him. She was younger than Thai, better looking than Thai, and having just broken off her engagement with Dave, who lived on the other side of the gulf, she was available.

On the rare occasions when Silas came close enough to the car, Steve would nod in his direction. *Linin' it all up, mate. Any day now.*

Silas could see how glazed Shelley's eyes were, and how quickly Steve had turned away, but he couldn't be bothered to respond, and as Steve came to sense that Silas was absorbed elsewhere, he stopped making any attempts to acknowledge what was still owing.

But Thai refused to give in. Chain-smoking on the verandah, she would drum her fingers, the nails bitten down red-raw, barely glancing up when Silas asked her a question about Rudi and Constance.

What the fuck would I know? she snapped once, slapping at a mosquito, the smear of blood red on her forearm. *He's a fuckin' madman who keeps his daughter locked up.*

It was the only thing she ever said about Rudi, and what she had to say about Constance amounted to even less.

Never seen her, and Thai stood up abruptly, her body thin and sharp in the moonlight, each muscle tensed at the sound of Steve's car, pulling up outside the pub.

Might just have to nick off for a few minutes. She smiled at Silas for the first time in days, a look of cunning flickering across her face. *Reckon you could look after the kids?* She touched his arm briefly, in an attempt to convince him she was the relaxed earth mother she would have liked him to believe she was, and then she was gone, her silver bracelets clicking back and forth as she loosened her hair from the thin scraggly knot at the base of her neck and crossed the dirt yard.

The boys stared up at Silas. The youngest girl, Sass, sucked her thumb, a dirty T-shirt clutched in one hand, while the older one, Jade, continued chopping the hair off her Barbie doll.

When are you meant to go to bed? Silas asked her.

She shrugged her shoulders. *No time.*

Want to go for a swim?

They stared at him.

Where? Lucas asked, a wide grin cutting across his face.

Where do you reckon? Silas pointed out to where the jetty stretched towards the horizon, splicing straight and sure through the black night-time waters of the gulf.

He scooped Sass up in his arms and reached for Jade, the two boys dancing around him and giggling.

We got no swimmers, and Lucas smirked at the sheer lunacy of the idea.

Who cares?

As they crossed the dirt road and turned right towards the jetty, Silas asked them questions. It was information on Constance that he wanted, anything they knew, and as they quickly sensed his eagerness for answers, Eli indicated that he wanted a rollie, Lucas, ten dollars, before they would tell him anything, both of them running circles around him, both of them holding out their hands in expectation of their bribes.

Sass was asleep when they reached the thin strip of weed-littered sand, all that was left of the expanse of beach that had glared under the hot daytime sun. Silas laid her down on his towel, and, asking the question again, he gave each of the boys the payment he had promised.

They stared at him, faces blank.

Well?

Eli started miming, his thin hands moving rapidly, the expressions on his face exaggerated, as Lucas watched him intently. Silas could only wait for the translation, impatient with the game they still insisted on playing.

Yes? And he looked at Lucas, who had the ten dollars clutched firmly in one hand.

He just stared back.

What was he saying?

Lucas turned to his brother for an instant and then back to Silas. *Nothin',* his voice was loud and clear, almost sweet in its innocence and then he pulled his T-shirt off over his head, eager to get in the water.

Silas tried to snatch the money from his grasp, but Lucas was too quick, skinny legs flashing white in the darkness as he squealed in excitement at the possibility of a new game. Eli stayed sitting next to Jade, attempting to roll the cigarette, the tobacco spilling out the ends, as he glanced up briefly, warily.

What were you saying to him? Silas asked.

He just looked down, his concentration focused on the piece of paper in his hand.

Silas sighed in exasperation. There was no point. He would float out in the cool, salty water, the moonlight spilling across his body, and attempt to make up his own answers to the questions he had.

Wait right here, he made them promise, wishing he had never brought them in the first place, and he pointed to the cigarette in Eli's hand, *or I'll tell your mum you nicked it from me.*

He paddled slowly, feeling his way through the black water, listening to the slap of the sea against the pylons, Lucas's whoops of joy from the shore and, from further out, the occasional murmur of voices, Mick and Jason, fishing in the darkness.

With his eyes closed, Silas did not hear it or see it before he felt it, the rip of the hook against his shorts, and the sharp splice of the twine against his flesh as he struggled to break free.

Jesus, and his voice rang out in the silence. *Jesus,* his splashing was furious as he tried to look up.

He could hear them laughing and the twang as one of them pulled a ring can, flicking it down to where he struggled below them.

Gottya, Jason laughed, but it was Mick who looked over the railing.

Watch it, his words a whisper in the quiet.

— 5 —

When Silas failed to show up at the library, Greta became anxious.

He was always there, she told me later.

She was aware of a concern she felt for him, a slight unease each day he didn't come in, his boots loud on the hard floor as he passed her, looking across to give her a quick grin as he slid into his seat. She occasionally contemplated going to his place to see if he was all right but she was, as always, slightly uneasy at the thought of seeing him outside the safe routine they had established together.

And then, after three days of wondering where he was, she saw that he was back. She looked up to notice him pushing the heavy doors open as the late afternoon sun was slanting through the high windows, the thin streams of light making it difficult for her to see him clearly as he made his way, hurriedly, towards her desk.

She did not have enough time to conceal the shock. *You look terrible,* she told him, her voice a whisper in the quiet.

He nodded towards the exit and she glanced at her watch. There was only half an hour until closing.

I have to finish, and she flicked through the thick wad of pages she still hadn't read. She only had a couple of months of pay left on the project and she was a long way behind.

Please, and the urgency in Silas's voice startled her.

Outside, in the warmth of the sun, they sat side by side on the library steps, and Greta waited for Silas to speak.

It's getting worse. He lit a cigarette, his hand shaking as he put the match out, his sleeve pushed up just enough for her to see the latest damage he had inflicted upon himself.

She was, she told me, at a loss as to how to respond. *Have you talked to Daniel?* As he shook his head, she wished he had other friends.

She put her hand across her throat, aware of Silas's eyes on her again, and wanting to cover the softness of her skin near the top of her breast, because she suddenly felt uncomfortable at the memory of the night they had spent together, flitting at the edge of each conversation they had.

I can't help you, and Greta shook her head. *I'm just not able to.*

I know, and he shifted slightly, moving away from her, breathing in before he continued because there was something he wanted to say, she could see it.

When I was away, there was someone I met. His words were hesitant and she could tell he hated his inability to pick the exact ones he needed.

And I fucked up badly.

She, too, had inched away from him. *We've all done that.*

He shook his head. *Badly.*

She did not know if she wanted him to continue, but when he reached for her, she knew he was trying to let her know that it was all right. He was not going to do or say anything that would damage the tentative beginnings of the friendship they had constructed, and she felt herself relax, slightly.

If something I did caused all that's happening to me now, then I just don't see how I can expect to fix it by seeing Daniel. He can't take back what happened.

Greta did not understand. She looked at him. *But that's not what you are seeing him for.*

Silas stubbed out his cigarette. He pushed up his sleeves, not bothering to hide the full extent of the damage from her. Greta stood up. She stepped backwards down the stairs to street level, and he did not follow her, nor did he call her back. She looked towards one end of the road and then to the other. She unknotted her cardigan from her waist and wrapped it around her shoulders. He was watching her as she made her way towards him again, her arms wrapped tight around her chest, the glare now gone from the sun so that behind him, the façade of the library was becoming little more than a darkness.

She picked up her bag. *I have to get my things. They'll be closing soon.*

He didn't try to stop her.

She rubbed at her temple and stared at the ground. He bent his head so that he could catch her gaze from where he sat, knees to his chest, there on the step below the one on which she was standing.

Am I too much of a mess? His smile was rueful, but his eyes were serious.

For what?

For a friendship.

No, and she was surprised to find herself uttering what she had always known was inside her, a trust in him, despite what had passed. *But you need to talk to Daniel, or someone.*

I know.

As she reached down to help him up, his hand warm in her own, she realised how much she had missed seeing him around.

I guess it was then that I knew, she told me later.

What? I asked her.

That I had fallen for him, and she smiled as she looked down at the table. *I just hadn't wanted to admit it to myself.*

I watched as she bit her lip.

You know what he's like.

I told her that I did.

⁓ 6 ⁓

When I went to Port Tremaine, I saw that Thai's house was just as Silas had described it: a double-fronted wooden cottage that was slowly collapsing into the earth, the dry paint flaking off in great strips of pale blue, the colour fading to a dirty white.

There were still toys in the front yard: broken plastic cars, a decapitated doll, a water pistol, all littered across the dust. If I hadn't heard she had moved, I would have thought the place was occupied. Torn curtains hung in the windows and the front door was open, hanging on one hinge only.

Packed up about a year ago, Pearl had told me.

She had not let me into the shop. We had conducted our conversation through the flyscreen door. *Closed up,* she had explained, *too old for this carry-on,* and she had indicated the rows of sagging dust-covered shelves behind her, still stacked with boxes and tins, mostly food, all of which would have been well past their use-by date.

I walked around Thai's house, looking into each of the empty rooms, wanting to see it as it would have been when

Silas was there over four years ago. The cottage out the back, where he had stayed, was still furnished. The single bed was covered in mouse droppings; the stuffing was bursting out of the mattress. On the floor was a pile of paperbacks, the pages yellowed and water-stained, the covers bent back and torn. I wondered whether they had been Silas's, left behind in his rush to get out of there, and as I picked one of them up, moths fluttered out, tiny, blind and white, their wings beating furiously as they attempted to make it towards the light from the window.

Outside Silas's mother's house, I saw the bath. It was rusted through, leaning lopsided on the one leg that remained. I did not go any further than the door. Not only was the floor collapsed, the smell caused me to pull back. Peering into the darkness, I could just make out the bulk of an animal, a wallaby I presume, the flies thick around its rotten carcass, and I stepped back into the brightness of the day with relief.

Walking around the building, I saw that it was one of the largest houses in the town and one of the oldest. Silas's guess that this was where his mother had come for holidays was probably correct. Wealthy rural families had owned a few of the places here. It was hardly a glamorous seaside resort but it would have provided a brief period of respite from the unrelenting heat of the summers in the country that lies beyond the ranges.

Silas had no idea how often she had visited this place or when she had stopped, but this was not surprising. He knew little about her life before her marriage.

We didn't touch on anything for long, he told me once. *We never went beyond a light-hearted banter, the kind of social chit-chat that you might have at lunch when you are trying to amuse each other.*

Whenever I asked him about his father, he would look out the window and tell me they'd had little in common. I do not know whether this was the way it had always been or whether Silas's shame at his father's business activities had caused this breakdown. It may have been that the possibility of any kind of relationship had been too severely hindered by his father's delusions; he never told me.

I do know that Silas's father died shortly after his return from Port Tremaine. I read the articles in the paper, the features written by various investigative journalists that attempted to unravel where the money had gone, the diagrams that marked out the numerous trust funds, some of which Silas was the sole beneficiary, many others of which were tied up for years in the control of various solicitors and shelf companies. It was all so complex that later, when I was treating him, I did not wonder at Silas's inability to deal with it.

Silas did not go to either his mother's or his father's funeral.

I should have gone to hers, he told me. *I missed her,* and he looked down at the floor. *I had so little to fix me to the ground, to the world, I suppose.* He shifted in his chair.

Losing her had shaken him. She was that one thread, a very fine one, I know, that had linked him to the earth, and when she died, he had felt there was nothing, no matter where he was, to keep him steady.

belladonna

Belladonna

Clinical. – – Atropa Belladonna. Deadly Nightshade.

Characteristics. – – *Belladonna* acts primarily on the brain, and Teste very acutely explains the diversity of its action on men and animals by suggesting that it acts with an intensity proportionate to the brain development. On goats and rabbits it has no poisonous action whatever. On carnivorous animals it acts with moderate intensity. On man it acts with highest intensity. But on idiots, as Hufeland mentions, it has no more action than it has on some of the carnivora.

John Henry Clarke, *A Dictionary of Practical Materia Medica*

— 1 —

It took an hour to walk to the garden. Silas went each morning, leaving as soon as he woke, the heat in his room unbearable by eight o'clock, particularly after long nights of smoking and drinking with the others on the verandah.

The sand was on fire beneath his feet as he followed the track that skirts the edge of the mangrove swamps, the mud rank to the smell, rich and rotting, before he turned inland, into the low-lying scrub, desert brush, saltbush and gorse all scratching at his flesh, scoring red crisscrosses on his skin, tiny pin-pricks of blood to mark where he had been.

This was when he was alone; he was not at Thai's with the kids screaming around him, he was not at Pearl's, drawing out the tales he knew she wanted to spin, and he was not at Rudi's, pressed against the wall by the constant flood of words. For that hour he did not see anyone, and in the absence of all eyes but his own, he did not know who he was or what he was doing in this place.

But when he came down the slight dip in the hill and saw the sunlight hot on the metal fencing and beyond, that garden holding within it the promise of Constance, his pace would quicken.

It was beautiful, he tried to explain when he first began talking to me about it. *Mesmeric,* and he would stumble for words to do it justice.

There was that town and then that place. Two completely different worlds. In one, everything was dying and in the other, I had never seen so much life. But strange life. Plants I had never seen before – fleshy tubular flowers, sticky stamens, gaping mouths, drooping heads; it was like a dream, and Silas looked at the ceiling in disbelief at what he was trying to express. *A sort of terrible caricature of a Freudian nightmare.*

I smiled. *The worst kind.*

All he wanted was a few moments alone with Constance, and each day, when Rudi let him in, he would look for her, remaining hopeful despite the fact that they had still only exchanged a few words.

He was surprised when, about three weeks after his first visit, she was simply there at the gate, keys in hand, Rudi nowhere in sight. The problem was that he found himself unable to speak. His throat was dry from the heat, and he brushed at the flies that gathered in a thick swarm as he tried to summon the words he had imagined.

He's waiting for you, she said, and stepped aside, indicating that he should walk as he always walked, up the path that led to the shack.

It's you I'd like to see, he told her.

Her words were direct as she snapped the padlock closed. *What for?*

He could not think of an appropriate reply. It was simply that he was obsessed with her, lifted high on a glittering wave of infatuation, so high that he felt dizzy with the sensation.

Do you want me in your article as well?

He had forgotten the story he had used and, once again, he was relieved she could not see his embarrassment. He told her he wanted her to show him the garden, he wanted to know how she made it all grow, why she had done it, what kind of a life she led, his questions tumbling out in an excited rush.

I want to know it all. He was relieved to see the faintest smile on her face. *If you've got the time.*

As her smile deepened, she appeared, for a moment, like a child. The wariness dissolved, and all Silas wanted was to hold this moment still.

Maybe you could start by showing me your favourite, the one you love, the flower you are always with, and, forgetting once again that she could not see, he pointed towards the softness of the silky cream petals folding across each other, their smell heady in the heat. *Or any of them, I don't mind.*

The light was dancing in her eyes so that they shone, like moonstones, as she listened to him.

And then maybe I could show you what it's like out there, and he leant forward, his tone more serious now, urgent. *Because you don't have to stay here. There is so much to see. We could do it. Just open that gate again and keep going.*

Any levity in her expression dissipated. She stepped back, and Silas knew he had said too much.

There is nothing wrong with my life. Her voice was low.

I know, Silas rushed to apologise, reaching for her, her skin cool beneath his touch.

Besides, and she brushed his hand away, *I am blind. Showing me the world would be pointless.* Her last words were almost a whisper in the silence that had descended – the branches of the trees overhead were suddenly still, the slow sway of the flowers, the rustle of the leaves, the flicker of insects were all gone in that moment -- and they both stood, apart again.

I am sorry, Silas said. *I don't want to upset you.*

She had a leaf in her fingers, and she twirled it, back and forth, in a rapid blur of brilliant green. He reached out to still her, but she seemed to sense his presence and moved away.

I don't know what came over me, he told her, wanting only to see her smile again, *I was just trying to get to know you. I didn't think.* Her expression had not changed. *I'm quite happy just to be here,* he insisted. *I'm not being patronising. I want to learn from you.* There was a desperation to his words now. *All I've ever done is make a complete mess of my life out there. I need to change. I want to change.* He did not know what he was saying. He was only aware of the distance that had grown between them, and the limited time he had before Rudi came, once again, to claim him. *Please,* he asked, *can't you trust me?*

Constance let go of the leaf she had been holding. *He deserves respect,* and she nodded in the direction of the shack. *He believes he will finally be recognised again.*

Silas glanced down the path, fearful that Rudi was making his way towards them.

I know, and he could only think to lie to her. *I will do what I can to write something that will be read.*

It could have been the heat, or the amount he had drunk the previous evening alone in his room, or perhaps it was the richness of the scent that clung to her skin; it did not matter what had caused it, but he felt faint, and he held onto the nearest tree in an attempt to steady himself.

Don't make a fool of him.

As he sunk to the ground, he reached for her. *I am sorry,* he said. *I probably just need a drink of water.*

Her hand was cool and dry around his wrist as she told him to hush, to be still, it would pass. *Just close your eyes.*

He leant forward, his palms pressed against his face, and that was when he felt it, the stickiness of the warm blood trickling between his fingers. It was just his nose, that was all it was, and he looked at the red stain on his skin.

Here. She was right there by his side, her sweetness overpowering, and she was holding a flower, a rose-pink blossom, spread open against the whiteness of her palm. *Go on,* and she pressed it closer.

He would have done anything she asked.

Periwinkle, she told him, a slight smile once again tracing the corners of her lips. *Used for hysteria.* As she helped him up, he saw the amusement in her eyes. *Witches have been known to put them in love potions, but they are also very good for nosebleeds.*

As he crushed the petals into his mouth, he wondered how she had known what was wrong with him, and he looked across at her in wonder.

Can you help me up? he asked, wanting to feel her touch again.

She told him to stay as he was for a few more moments, and because she seemed to be about to turn away, he opened his mouth to speak again, wanting only to hold her there with him.

So everything, all of this, and he indicated the garden as he searched for a question, a comment, anything to get her attention, *has a use, a purpose?*

Her smile was wry now. *It depends on what you mean by purpose.*

Do you use them all for healing?

She turned her face towards the sun, now high overhead. *There's not a lot of people who come here to be healed.*

But he used to treat people, and, without thinking, Silas

nodded in the direction of the shack, aware as soon as he did so that she could not see his gesture.

She was facing him directly now and there was a hardness in her expression he had not noticed before. *That was a long time ago.*

What happened? Silas asked. *To the others?*

She tapped her toe against a rock, the sound repetitive and harsh in the quiet. *There's nothing mysterious about any of it. There were disagreements and gradually they left. All of them. One by one.*

Silas held onto the trunk of the tree and pulled himself up. *But he decided to stay?*

She had turned away from him.

It must get lonely, it must be difficult, sometimes.

Not particularly. Her tone was sharp.

For him, Silas said, the memory of Rudi drunk, the first night he saw him, flashing across his thoughts.

You are in no position to judge. Your own capacity for consuming poisons hardly indicates a peace with the world.

If he was alarmed at her apparent ability to read his mind, he did not have a chance to let it register, the anger in her words increasing as she continued.

Do not presume to think you know what our life is like. You have come here for some unfathomable reason that has nothing to do with us and you are simply seeing what you want to see.

Silas did not know what to say. He ran his foot through the

soil, wishing he could win her trust, but each time he tried, it seemed to go wrong. *I am not what you think I am,* he said.

I have no idea who you are, she told him. *I can't see you.*

No, he protested. *You've made up your mind. You won't give me a chance. But I keep coming back because I really do want to know. I want to know you.*

She was rolling up her sleeves so that she could return to her work. He just looked at her in silence, but her face gave nothing away.

How's your nose? she eventually asked, and he watched as she felt across the dirt, her fingers tapping lightly as she searched for the trowel she had been using before she had let him in.

He touched his face. *Better,* and at the risk of causing yet another rift, he asked her how she had known.

To use the periwinkle?

No, that I was bleeding.

She grasped the trowel and dug into the soil, her hair falling across her face as she turned towards him.

My powers, she told him.

With the darkness of her hair hiding her expression, he was uncertain as to whether she was smiling.

My very strange powers.

And as he reached across to help her stake the seedlings at their feet, he realised he had no idea whether she was joking or not.

— 2 —

When Silas asked me to explain how the remedy I had given him could work, I told him he needed to throw away notions he held as truths; he needed to see the world in a different way.

He tried. I know. When he sat in the library, with his eyes half closed, he was not only wanting to capture the way in which Constance saw, he was also reaching for a broader understanding, he was trying to bring a new vision of the world within his own reach.

When I ask you questions, I once tried to explain, *I am attempting to draw out the inner expression of the defence mechanism. I need to see both the totality of the symptoms and those that are rare or peculiar in order to form a complete picture. The remedy we pick will have the same essence or nature as this expression.*

Silas could not understand how you could see such a thing, unless of course you had the vision supposedly possessed by Constance, the capacity to see the field, the extraordinary dancing charge that surrounds everything.

In his articles, Rudi would always talk about the soul of

a remedy. This was, in fact, the phrase he used in several of his conversations with Silas.

It is a question of knowing, and Rudi would turn excitedly to where Constance worked, silently, at the other end of the shack.

It is extraordinary, and he would lean forward, unable to suppress his amazement, *her ability to actually see the essence of it all. Everything.*

Once, Silas told me, Rudi had knocked his tea over in his enthusiasm, the liquid spreading, pale brown, across his notes. *She can look at you and she can know what remedy it is that you need – just like that.* The click of his fingers had made Constance start. Silas saw it, the slight jerk in her shoulders as she had continued working.

I cannot tell you what that means, and Rudi had sighed. *I cannot tell you what I would give, just to know what she sees,* and from the other end of the room, Silas had heard the grinding of the pestle against the mortar, the slight break in the rhythm as Constance had listened to her father's words.

The essential nature. A flower, a tree, a stone, a piece of grass, a venom; the list of potential substances with therapeutic properties is infinite. We just have to know them, we just have to be able to see, and without Constance's vision, we are left with a need to conduct provings such as this one.

When Larissa and Matthew commence taking the remedy we are examining, I will be overseeing their case on a daily basis and I must be observant of all alterations that occur; I cannot rely on what they tell me alone. From the little I know of this process (I have only ever participated in informal provings in the past, occasionally trying remedies on myself), the provers can become the proving and therefore may not know that they are experiencing change. If we were testing Scorpion they would become the Scorpion, right there in the centre of their beings. They would feel that all they were experiencing was perfectly normal, they would tell me that there had been no change (unless, of course, the symptoms were particularly blatant or physical), because the part of them that observes would also be Scorpion, blind to its own nature.

What interests me, and it is a phenomenon that Rudi wrote about extensively, is to do with the notion of a collective unconsciousness. Because we are talking about energy here, and we are therefore discarding boundaries as we have been taught to construct them, it would not be surprising to find that those of us who are participating in this proving without taking the remedy experience related symptoms. I, for example, may have similar physical, mental and emotional sensations to those experienced by the provers in our group. So, too, may the other supervisors, perhaps even the director, despite her not being here with us.

When he wrote about this, Rudi always took it one step

further. There have been others who have written similar articles, who have described related phenomena occurring on a larger world scale during a proving process. For example, during the proving of hydrogen, two scientists with no knowledge of the testing being conducted announced that they had achieved nuclear fusion at room temperature. Three months later, as the proving neared completion, the claim was announced to be false, but three years later, when the results of the proving were published, a similar claim was again made. A colleague of mine was once involved in the proving of a particular bark. As the proving commenced, a blockade was announced to prevent woodchipping of those trees. I have heard of various diseased tissues being tested at the same time as supposed breakthroughs in the treatment of the particular diseases were announced; they are all random stories and when I hear them, I am torn between dismissing them as pure coincidence and feeling a strange excitement at the possibilities they open up.

I told Silas to throw away notions he held as truths, and he tried. There are times when I have to tell myself this as well. It is something we all need to do. Because it is only then that whole new worlds begin to unfold in front of us, sometimes beautiful, sometimes terrifying, sometimes both at once, depending on how far we are prepared to let go, how willingly we take the leap.

— 3 —

Sometimes, in the peace of the library, Silas tried to write a list. He would open his notebook, a blank page, smooth and white on the desk in front of him, wanting to itemise what it was that had led him to become obsessed with Constance in the way he had. There were distinct circumstances he could write down: Pearl's stories; the amount he had smoked; his isolation in that town; the very strangeness of the garden and the lives Rudi and Constance led; his mother's death . . . He could list them all, maybe more if he thought for longer, but it was never going to be enough.

Greta told me she had seen some of his lists.

But as I got to know him better, I stopped doing it. Prying, that is, and she looked away in embarrassment, both of us realising that we were circling a discussion neither of us was sure about commencing, even though we knew that it was the real reason for meeting up again, despite the fact that we had spent most of the morning talking about Silas.

You know I am sorry, Greta said.

Don't, I interrupted her.

Do you know, Greta asked me, *what he wrote, at the end of each of those lists?*

I thought for a moment that we had gone back to the safe topic, the one on which we had been lingering, the topic of Silas, and I was relieved. I shook my head.

'*Myself*', and Greta looked at me. *He would cross everything else out and that was all that would be left.*

There's no need, I told her.

For what?

For you to say that it was all your fault.

But it was, and she just looked at me, squarely, directly, as I attempted to meet her gaze.

4

Silas told me that if he could have got to a doctor, he would have. If there had been someone who would have driven him up to the tip of the gulf and then down to the town on the other side where the leaden smoke belches out of the stacks by the wharves, he would have asked to be taken there, the words dry on his cracked lips. But in the rare moments of lucidity that came in between the hours of being rocked mercilessly by a fever of extraordinary intensity, he knew he had little hope of finding outside help.

It had begun as a dizziness, a sensation almost sparkling, dazzling, in its purity. He had stopped and leant against the trunk of the soap mallee that grew at the end of the dirt track leading into town, the illness now rolling in, great waves washing through him. Five minutes later, as he stumbled across the road towards Thai's, his teeth were chattering and his vision was blurred. He was freezing cold, the sweat on his forehead was like ice melting, and in his mouth was the taste of the flower Constance had given him, peppery and dry.

Can you help me? he called out to the older girl, Jade, who was digging graves for all her dolls beneath his window, but either no words came out or she didn't hear him. She had used Paddle-pop sticks for each of the crosses, and as he tried to make a feeble joke about the number of ice-creams she must have eaten, he passed out, his legs folding beneath him, his body crumpling onto the floor.

It was three days before he made it out of his bed. Leaning against the door, he could only just see Thai, her outline fuzzy as he looked out into the brilliance of the day.

Jesus, mate, you had us worried, and as she shook her head, Silas tried to recollect any moments during his illness when she had exhibited concern. It had been Lucas who had brought in the cracked cups filled with water, still there by his bed, and the two bowls of tinned spaghetti, also still there, the pasta dried to the edge of the plate.

He was surprised at how weak he was and how he had to lean on Thai's shoulder, her bones sharp and hard against his arm, when he attempted to walk. She led him out of his room and across the dirt to her place, Steve bending down and hoisting him up onto the verandah.

Back in the land of the living?

Silas pulled back from the sweet staleness of Steve's breath, wet smoky grass, pungent as he leant a little closer to pass Silas the joint he had been smoking, the tip soggy to the touch.

Deal finally came through, and he patted the bag next to him, half of which he had already smoked with Shelley.

Thai let out a thin exhalation of smoke, her chin tilted upwards, her eyes narrowed. She glanced across at Silas briefly, her words muttered just loud enough for him to hear — *and a certain someone has gone back to her bloke* — as she tossed the dead match across the yard.

If Steve heard, he did not show it. He just pushed the bag over and asked her to roll them another.

With his back against the wall, Silas closed his eyes. Splinters of dry wood were pricking through his T-shirt, but he did not move. He could feel the warmth of the sun creeping along his legs and he hoped that somehow it was instilling enough strength into his limbs for him to eventually pull himself up and head back out along the track to Rudi's. He could hear Steve drawing in the last of the joint with a sharp intake of breath, and letting it out again with a slight whistle. Steve was watching Silas or, at least, that was what Silas presumed, because when he opened his eyes, the sunlight dazzling, he saw that Steve had turned in his direction, his expression unreadable behind the black wraparound glasses he always wore.

Want a word of advice, mate? He was going to give it whether Silas wanted it or not. *Hanging around up there — it's what they call a health hazard.*

He nodded in what Silas could only guess was the

direction of Rudi's, and because he could feel the joint that Steve had handed him starting to burn between his fingers, he held it up to his lips, the paper hot on the end of his tongue. He looked at them both and then beyond them to the dirt, the few scrappy sand mallees out on the road, and out to the ranges, burnt orange under the clear blue sky.

Steve's comment had not surprised him. It was a thought that had crossed his own mind. There had been moments during his fever when he had wondered whether she had wanted to make him ill, and he had tossed around in his bed, his dreams punctuated by images of Constance and the flower she had given him. He smiled to himself. It was a ludicrous notion, but there was a drama to it, an intensity that matched the passion with which she had countered any of the comments he had made concerning the way in which she lived, and he smiled to himself because there was, in his exhausted state, something almost appealing about the idea. He shook his head.

Here we are again. He was surprised at the sound of his own voice; it was remarkably unchanged, despite every part of his being feeling as though it had been through a fire and back again.

Yep indeed, and Thai held up the joint she had just rolled, admiring its perfection for a few moments before handing it over to Steve.

Yep, Silas repeated sometime later, uncertain as to how

much time had actually passed since anyone had spoken. *Ever been out there?* He turned towards Steve, his words so slurred that he wasn't sure whether they were intelligible.

When Steve finally responded about five minutes later, Silas had forgotten what he had asked. *Tried to shoot me once.* He scratched at his beard. *Thought I was after his daughter,* and he shook his head in amazement. *Went there with Mick, shooting cans.* He grinned. *I was just talking to her, passin' the time of day, and fuck me dead if he wasn't out there with a gun pointed at me.*

Silas closed his eyes again, the dope curling down the back of his throat, creeping through his limbs. He wanted to pull himself up, jump off the verandah, the chickens squawking at his feet as he crossed the yard, and for a moment he could see himself, swinging each leg over the gate, the dirt on the road a dusty yellow cloud behind him. But he couldn't move.

Steve took a long swig of beer and then kicked the empty bottle onto the pile. *Any more, darl?* He looked across at Thai, her sharp face turned up towards the sun, her eyes closed.

Try the fridge, she told him, without looking in his direction.

The screen door slammed shut behind him when he returned. The boards shuddered beneath his weight as he settled back into his seat.

Jase reckons she threatened him with a snake one time. Told him she kept them as pets. Steve flicked the ring pull at Thai, thinking it would get her attention. A fine spray of beer sparkled across the verandah, but she did not move.

Silas had his hands pressed down, the wood dry beneath his skin, in an attempt to push himself up. It was extraordinary, there was no power in his body. He grinned to himself, staring at the feebleness of his arms, and he wondered, idly, whether this was in fact himself, or someone else, the real Silas far away from here. All he could do was close his eyes, a faint smile disturbing the stillness of his face, Steve's words floating out there around him.

I mean, mate, you're hanging around there, you're sick as a dog; it all adds up.

Silas just nodded, not sure what added up anymore.

Friendly advice, that's all it is.

If he tried hard, Silas could see her, the paleness of her skin, the thick cloud of dark hair.

She knows everything, he said dreamily, uncertain as to whether he had, in fact, spoken out loud.

They were just a type of belladonna, she had told him, the flowers she loved the most. The atropine was used by women to dilate their pupils. *To make them more attractive,* and a smile had curved at the corners of her lips.

Her long white fingers had scrabbled in the soil. *Mandragora.*

He had kept pointing to them all, wanting to know what

they were, but also just wanting to keep her there with him.
A cluster of creamy-yellow cup-shaped flowers, heavily
veined with purple, and he had bent down to touch the yellow fruit that lay on the ground. It was pulpy, rotting into
the earth, moist beneath his hands.

It's the roots that we use, and she had shown him. They were
human in shape, a male figure, there in her hold.

She had smiled at him then, a full smile, alive with mis-
chief, as she had stepped back from the hole she had dug,
both hands clasped over her ears. *The shriek.*

He had no idea what she meant.

If you pull them from the ground they shriek.

All he had wanted was to kiss her.

*Anyone who hears the shriek of a mandrake root dies. That's
what they used to believe. They used to dig all around the root and
then tie a dog to it by a string. When the master called the dog, the
dog would run towards him and pull the root out. Then it would die.
Just like that,* and she had clapped her hands, the sound harsh
in the quiet.

He wanted to get back to her.

He opened his eyes and saw the ash on his skin from
where the joint had burnt down, the last of the paper, grey
and sodden, between his middle and forefinger.

Mate, and Thai handed him another.

He just shook his head. *Think I might go for a walk,* and as
he pressed his hand down onto the verandah, a fly settled on

his mouth. He swiped at it, his whole body slumping again. Later, he thought, and he closed his eyes, hoping she was still there; Constance, right inside his head, exactly where he had left her.

— 5 —

Shortly after Silas first mentioned that he had been in love with Constance, he tried to qualify what he meant. He told me that even then he knew it was ridiculous to talk of love when he did not know her, when he had rarely talked to her alone; not that love was a word anyone was using, not even Pearl, and she was the only one who had begun to guess at the true extent of his feelings, she was the only one to whom he really talked.

In the dusty gloom of her shop, she said she'd heard that Constance had got *her hooks* into him, that he'd been spending all his time *mooning around up there*, she nodded in the direction of Rudi's place, *and look where it's got you. Hardly a picture of health*.

She held her crochet up for a moment, throwing the full size of the lurid rug across the clutter that covered the counter. Sometimes it was necessary to look at the complete pattern in order to choose the next layer, and her eyes widened as she took in the sickly rings of pea green, mauve and fluorescent yellow. Silas waited, his gaze fixed in fascination on the pink pudginess of her fingers as she snipped the wool with a pair of rusted scissors and knotted on the next ball.

She leant forward, her watery blue irises magnified beneath the thick glasses she wore.

Have you seen them? she asked.

Seen what? Silas brushed at a fly, his hand momentarily getting caught in the tangles of colour spilling across the teapot, teacup, sugar and cashbox.

The snakes she keeps.

He pulled back. *Really?*

This was what he came for, pushing the heavy door open each morning, his eyes adjusting to the darkness, the stale sweetness of old sugar sickly in the air; he was eager for any information about her, and Pearl knew it, teasing it out, strand by strand.

Hundreds of them, and Pearl sniffed. *She's immune to them. It's the venom in her blood.*

Pearl was born out the back of the shop, and that was where she would die; *and there aren't many that can boast that.* It had been years since she'd walked any further than the few steps to the street out the front, dragging the heavy 'Open for Business' sign that she insisted on displaying each day, its legs clattering across the pavement. Yet despite her lack of mobility, she knew whatever there was to be known and, like Steve, she enjoyed imparting her knowledge.

Don't think anything escapes me, she had once told Silas and he had nodded solemnly.

I wouldn't dare. He had winked at her.

Cheekiness will get you nowhere, and she had rolled up a newspaper and taken a swipe at him.

Personally, and Silas leant a little closer, knowing that any obvious display of curiosity concerning her comment about the snakes would only protract the telling of the story even further, *I would have chosen a red,* and he shook his head as he pointed to the orange she had begun to integrate into the pattern.

Hmph. She pushed her glasses down to the tip of her nose.

She was about to speak, Silas could sense it, and he waited, ready for the next tantalising piece of information, when the door of the shop opened, the bell jangling in the momentary silence.

It was Mick, a can of Coke in one grease-stained hand, his money in the other. Silas turned to greet him, and was startled by the coldness of his glare. He had never noticed how green Mick's eyes were, but then most of the time Mick had worn his sunglasses and when he hadn't they had both been ripped, so it was not surprising he had failed to take in anything as mundane as eye colour. He let his hand fall to his side, stilled by the hostility in Mick's face.

It was Pearl who spoke. *Just been warning him about the snakes up at Rudi's,* and she nodded in Silas's direction.

She's been telling me tales, Silas added by way of friendly explanation.

Mick just grunted.

Pearl snorted. *I've been telling him he shouldn't spend so much time up there,* and she held out her hand for the money.

Mick let it drop, coin by coin, into her cashbox, without looking at either of them. When he finally spoke, the mutter of his words was so low, Silas was forced to lean closer. *Could have told him that myself.*

6

The first time Silas attempted to talk about the wounds on his arms, I am sorry to say the slightest flicker of agitation crossed my face. It was the frustration of being well into a treatment and realising there was still so much more to unearth. This is not uncommon, but with Silas, I felt particularly anxious about having failed to see what was, without doubt, the most worrying aspect of his condition.

This morning, collecting firewood with Jeanie and Sam (who still insists on being wherever I am), I spoke a little of Silas. As we stacked the last of the kindling into the wheelbarrow, she commented, once again, on my distance over these few days.

It's only because I'm concerned about you, she said.

Jeanie was once my teacher; she has also treated me several times and she knows me well. I have even stayed on her property, a small piece of land west of the mountains, where I amused her greatly with my complete lack of practical skills, only to make up for it with my ability to grasp the art of doing cryptic crosswords after only one brief lesson. She never fails to speak directly, and she is someone to whom I find it difficult to lie.

I told her I had needed some time in which to think, that I had been working too hard for too long. I smiled. *I guess I've forgotten how to relate to others.*

She just looked at me.

And there is personal stuff, I admitted, but it was Silas that I told her about, not Greta, and as I described the wounds he had inflicted upon himself, she listened.

Was it a desire for attention? she asked.

I shook my head and said I didn't think so.

When Silas first told me what he did, it was as though he had rehearsed his statement – when the problem began, how often it occurred and how long it lasted. Unusually, he looked directly at me as he spoke, his voice was well modulated, and his words were carefully chosen.

I listened without taking notes, and when he had finished, I asked him to tell me a bit more about his awareness, or lack of awareness, of the pain he was inflicting upon himself.

The irritation was immediate.

I told you, and his gaze was once again averted from mine. *I have no idea what's going on. I am asleep when it happens. This is pointless,* and he crossed and uncrossed his legs. *I would be better off seeing a psychiatrist.*

You could if you felt it would help.

He was silent for a few moments.

I apologised for pressing the point again. *What I'm trying to do is to get you to describe what happens to you — not what other people have told you that you do, but your impressions.* I could see the consternation on Silas's face. *I'm not so interested in what's caused this.* I wanted him to understand me. *It has some relevance but less than you would think. What I'm wanting is the particulars of what actually occurs from your perspective. That's what I need from you if we're going to make any progress.*

Silas rolled up a sleeve past the elbow, high until the folds were tight against his flesh, and then he pushed it higher. He held out his arm, the pale underside up. The bruises had yellowed and the cuts had healed over; thick scabs covered his wrist, lower arm, elbow and upper arm, the crust still new enough to reveal an open sore should he tear it away again without realising in the middle of the night. He did not look at the wounds and he did not look at me.

They were bad.

I told him it looked like he had been giving himself a difficult time, and my smile was rueful as I glanced straight up again. *I do need you to try to tell me what you remember feeling, thinking, seeing, hearing — anything at all from these episodes. If there's nothing, that's fine,* and I kept my eyes on Silas as I waited for an answer.

This was not what he had rehearsed. Silas pulled his sock

up and then pushed it down again. He did not like the territory we were entering and his discomfort was obvious.

How can the cause not be relevant? he asked.

I am more interested in the way your body has reacted, rather than why it has had this reaction. I could see he needed a better explanation. *You and I might both eat contaminated food. You might have mild stomach cramps, while I might be violently ill.*

He did not follow.

I reached for a book. *It's just a different way of looking at the world. A doctor would look at what caused my illness and then intervene. But your body has experienced little difficulty in adjusting to this outside influence, while my defence mechanism is producing certain signs and symptoms that doctors would call disease. That's what I am interested in, more so than what's caused the problem.*

I handed Silas a paperback and suggested he might like to read it. *It's a lay explanation.*

Silas put it down on the floor. I remembered how he had told me about the books Rudi had always pressed upon him (*you will need background information for your article*), and how each time he had left them behind.

I turned back to my computer. *It might be easier,* I said, *if I asked you a few questions.*

I don't know how much I can tell you. Silas looked at his hands, the nails bitten down, the skin scratched, and he sat on them, hiding them from view.

It could only be more than what you already have, and I raised an eyebrow as I smiled. *Do you have a sense that you are no longer lying in your bed asleep?*

Silas nodded.

Tell me about it.

What's there to tell? It's a sense, as you said.

It was one of the few moments I felt exasperated by him. *What kind of a sense? Do you notice a change in temperature, do you hear yourself shout, do you feel what you are doing to yourself?*

Silas shook his head.

But there is something?

He looked at his watch. The hour was just about up. I also checked how long was left, and I could not help but let out the faintest sigh as I, too, realised our time was almost over.

I'm not trying to be unhelpful, Silas told me.

I know.

I find it hard.

He turned to the window, fixing his eyes once again on the plumbing opposite.

I could not extend the appointment any longer. I was already running close to half an hour behind schedule but as he stood up, I reached for him, my fingers touching the wound on his wrist, alighting there briefly, but with a sense of purpose that could not be mistaken because I wanted him to hear me, I wanted him to trust.

You can't keep doing this to yourself.

And Silas just looked down at his feet.

7

There was a room in Silas's apartment where he put everything he no longer used. It had originally been his
grandmother's 'minor guest room', for guests she did not
really want to stay, guests whose continuing presence she
did not wish to encourage. Small and dark, with only one
window that looked out on another wall, it had housed a
single bed, a chest of drawers, and a tiny sombre oil paint-
ing. Now it was filled with boxes containing various scraps
of Silas's life.

Late one night, Silas unlocked the door. He had been
fearful of sleep, he told me, and he had decided to stay up.
He wanted to put all the different Silases that had existed
into separate piles. The young boy who wrote homesick letters to his mother; the period in which he had wanted
to understand why his parents lived as they did and his
father's unconvincing attempts at explaining how he had
been wronged, each letter more deluded than the last; the
documentation of his teenage rebellions – warning letters
from the schools he had attended, expulsion notices, even

a couple of court appearances for possession (both of which had been handled by his uncle, a QC); the love letters he had received; his school notes; his brief attempts at various businesses (importing carpets, jewellery, even setting himself up as an actor's agent), all of which had been abandoned when the amount of work involved had become evident. Within an hour he had laid out thirty-four different piles.

He sat on the floor and looked at them all.

How can you not know who you are? Constance had once said to him.

In the soft light of the garden, she had told him that this was who she was. *This,* and she had pointed to herself and then the plants that surrounded her.

He had thought she had a wholeness, a unity between herself and her environment that he had always longed for, a sense of stillness that had always eluded him.

Did she want more? He had no way of knowing.

What about company? he had asked. *Surely you must get lonely.*

She had blushed. He remembered. A slow, delicate wash of colour on her cheeks as she had turned to the wire fencing and stared, unseeing, out to the desolate country that lay beyond.

8

It was Eli who first commented on Silas's smell, the sickly sweetness that he had somehow grown used to, that had perhaps become so masked by the pungent reek of the dope he had been smoking that he barely noticed it. But when Eli wrinkled his nose in disgust, giggling to Lucas as he passed, Silas remembered the faintness of that smell as he had stood under the rusted shower rose that morning, the brown water drumming against the tin bath; the cloying odour that he had thought was the soap.

As he had begun to regain his strength, he tried, several times, to walk out to Rudi's. It had taken a week of attempts before he had finally got further than Pearl's and it was not until a few days later that he actually made it all the way out there. Each day he had got up early, wanting to leave the house before Thai woke, knowing that if she called him over to where she sat on the verandah, he would stop, thinking that just one smoke would be okay, and one would lead to two and soon the whole day would be wasted; her, Steve and him, sitting stupefied in the endless heat, and that was not what he wanted.

On that particular morning, Eli and Lucas were scratching a race track in the dirt, a great loop littered with makeshift Evel Knievel stunts – mounds of sand, lakes of water in upturned garbage lids, perilous troughs, and a half-constructed ring of fire.

He reckons you stink, Lucas told him, as if Eli's pinched nose and wrinkled mouth needed a translation. *Like a girl.*

Silas knelt down next to them and they pulled back in exaggerated disgust, the pair of them laughing now.

Pearl also commented on the odour. As the door clanged shut behind him, she glanced up from the corner of the shop where she always sat, her nose screwed up in distaste.

New aftershave?

Silas told her it was the soap he had been using.

Well, I'd change it if I were you, and she poured herself a cup of tea.

He watched as she searched for some sugar on the counter, only to find the jar was empty. She heaved herself up, breathing heavily as she pushed through the narrow gap at the side of the shelves.

Gone back to mooning around up there? She opened one of the packets for sale, spooned the sugar into her cup, and folded down the top before putting it back in the spot from which she had taken it.

Haven't seen the snakes yet, Silas told her.

She leant a little closer. *They obey her, you know. You cross her and they'll bite.*

The venom in her veins; Silas remembered Pearl's words.

She reached for the biscuits and dipped one into her cup. *Her mother was one of them. Hitchhiked out there just before they all started leaving.*

She licked the crumbs from the corner of her mouth, and Silas waited for more.

Last time I saw her, she was four months pregnant. Next I heard, she was bitten by a snake. She dunked the biscuit again, pausing as she sucked on it. *It was the shock that brought on the labour. Rudi wouldn't get her to a hospital and that child was born to a life with no mother and with poison in her blood. Little wonder she's not right in the head.*

Really? Silas reached for the fridge to get a can of Coke.

She nodded, her chin disappearing into the rolls of fat on her neck. *So you watch yourself, young man.*

I will, Silas promised.

And get yourself a new soap, she curled her top lip as he handed her the money for the drink. *Lux,* she pointed to the shelf.

Next time, Silas promised.

The door slammed shut behind him, and he stood for a moment, his arm held up to his nose, and breathed in deeply. They were right, he did smell. He looked out across the street, empty apart from Mick's dog, asleep under the shade of the bench outside the garage. It lifted its head lazily, noted his presence, and then closed its eyes again. In the dimness of the workshop, he could see Mick, and Silas raised his hand in greeting, letting it fall when he received no response. It was then, as the sweet smell lingered, thick in the heat, that he knew what it was. It was Constance, and he smiled to himself with the realisation.

Can't you tell? he asked her later, delighted to have found her, for the first time since his illness, by the gate without Rudi. He was holding his hand out to her, but she did not bend her head to test whether she had, as he had insisted, got under his skin; she just locked the gate again and turned to walk away.

Wait, and he held her arm, trying to stop her. She turned to him. *I am going to Rudi,* he promised. *I just wanted a few moments first.*

She told him she had tasks waiting for her.

You can stop for a little while, he urged, and he sat on the edge of a garden bed.

She remained standing.

Have you ever been swimming? he asked her.

She shook her head.

I go each night, Silas told her, wanting his words to keep her with him. *I just float out for miles. Last night I imagined what it would be like to take you.*

I can't swim.

Silas was relieved to see she was smiling slightly. *It doesn't matter. It is so salty that the water would carry you. I could hold my hand, just here,* and he curved his fingers into the small of her back, the fine ridges of her spine smooth beneath the cotton of her shirt, *and that would be enough.*

She moved away.

And the stars, Silas sighed. *They are spectacular. The sky is alive with them. They shimmer, tiny pocket-holes of light reflected back into the black of the gulf, dancing above and around you.*

Her words were direct as she reminded him once again that she could not see.

I'm sorry, he rushed to say, feeling the moment disintegrate, collapsing loose like powder between his fingers.

There's nothing to apologise for. It's just the way it is.

All that Silas wanted was for her to like him. *But sometimes it seems I have never been so hopeless at anything,* he told her ruefully. *What am I doing wrong?*

She was silent for a moment, the violet in her eyes cool as she considered his question.

I do like you, she said. *Is there some reason why I shouldn't?*

Silas did not know how to respond.

It was like that most of the time, he once told me, and he sighed, his face perplexed as he remembered. *She was always so matter of fact, so to the point, and I was such a ridiculous mess of emotion.*

Silas had been obsessed before, each time he fell in love in fact, but this was different.

I was at sea with it, completely out of my depth, and he looked away, the expression on his face one of shame. *I believed them,* he said, not looking at me.

What?

Those stories of Pearl's. That Constance had something, something that other people don't have, that I was ensnared, trapped, and he grinned in embarrassment as he shook his head. *I mean, I didn't, not really.* He rubbed his forehead with the back of his hand. *But I guess I did.*

— 9 —

All that I know of Rudi does not amount to much. In fact, until I met Silas, I did not even know he had a daughter. If, as Pearl told Silas, she was born shortly before the others started leaving, it would have been around the time that Rudi stopped publishing, otherwise he would, no doubt, have written about her and the vision she supposedly possessed.

His writings were, to say the least, eccentric, his beliefs unorthodox, and at the stage in my life when I discovered them, I thought they were extraordinary. I had just left medicine and even though my father thought I was a fool (he forgave everything except a lack of intellectual rigour, a deficiency that was defined, always, by his own standards), I felt my decision had been unquestionably right. I had discovered a way of thinking that made sense, and I wanted to take it to its outer reaches, to the places from which Rudi was writing.

Jeanie told me that she remembered recommending his articles. She always told her first-year students about them, and she always knew who would be amazed by them and who would find them barely worth the paper on which they were written.

It was like a game I played with myself, she smiled. *Working out those of you who were truly passionate, and those who weren't.*

She, too, had read the story of the redback spider. Apparently one had bitten Rudi, and the first thing he had demanded of the friend who found him was that he let him be; he wanted the venom to take its course and he wanted his friend to act as witness, to write down everything he said or did. Although the dosage was obviously toxic, the sensations he described were remarkable in their similarity to a recent orthodox proving of the spider that was conducted about a year ago.

You know he believed that simply holding the correct remedy in front of the patient could be enough?

I did.

And then he took it further. He tried to conduct trials to show that thinking of the remedy alone would suffice. She smiled. *He was absolutely obsessed, mad on one level, brilliant on another.*

As we wheeled the barrow back up to the house, I told her how I had gone out there to find him.

And did you?

I shook my head.

It was Pearl who had told me he had left. *Guess he didn't*

want to stay. She had rubbed her glasses with the cloth of her dress. *Not once she was gone,* and she had lifted a newspaper from the shelf near her and slammed it hard on the fly that had been buzzing, circling her head, while we talked.

s n a k e

Lachesis. – – . . . The Surukuku Snake of South America . . .
Characteristics. – – To the genius and heroism of Hering the
world owes this remedy and many another of which this has
been the forerunner. When Hering's first experiments were
made he was botanising and zoologising on the Upper
Amazon for the German Government. Except his wife, all
those about him were natives, who told him so much about
the dreaded Surukuku that he offered a good reward for
a live specimen. At last one was brought in a bamboo
box, and those who brought it immediately fled, and all his
native servants with them. Hering stunned the snake with a
blow on the head as the box opened, then, holding its head
in a forked stick, he pressed the venom out of the poison
bag upon sugar of milk. The effect of handling the virus and
preparing the lower attenuations was to throw Hering into
a fever with tossing delirium and mania – much to his
wife's dismay. Towards morning he slept, and on waking his
mind was clear. He drank a little water to moisten his throat
and the first question this indomitable prover asked was:
'What did I do and say?' His wife remembered vividly
enough. The symptoms were written down, and this was
the first instalment of the proving of *Lachesis*.

John Henry Clarke, *A Dictionary
of Practical Materia Medica*

— *1* —

The tide turns at Port Tremaine more quickly than one would ever expect. In the long, lazy heat of the day, the water might just reach the middle of the jetty, licking the bottom of the fourth set of stairs from the shoreline, leaving a wide stretch of weed-littered sand between the road that runs along the beach and the stillness of the gulf waters. Under the harshness of that sun, the air is thick with the rich, salty smell of rotting weeds as the brown and green clumps curl up, dry and brittle, and it seems impossible that there could ever be no beach, that the road could become the only border between town and sea.

Then the tide turns, swiftly, stealthily. The soft ripple of the water as it flows in leaves tiny fish flicking in a desperate attempt to fight against the pull of the current. Parched dry weeds flatten out into crescent strips of brown, black and glossy green as the ocean licks them, submerges them, swiftly creeping towards the third set of stairs and then the second and first, until it is soon covering a beach that once seemed too wide, too impossible a distance to traverse in order to reach the cool, cool sea.

That is when you get caught, if you aren't a local, if you aren't in the know. Visitors who come to fish drive their cars with boats in tow all the way to where the sea reaches the land, not realising how quickly it can turn, leaving them bogged or, if they are even more unlucky, submerged.

When the tide was right, Mick would close the garage early and take a few beers, plus the previous night's chops for bait, and spend the last hours of the day with Jason or Steve. They would sit on the bench that formed a barricade at the end of the jetty, the remaining few metres having washed away years earlier, and cast their lines out to where the pylons rear haphazardly out of the clear depth of the sea.

They were usually the first to see the few outsiders that ever came to this place. They would watch them pull up in their cars, look out across the gulf and then decide to drive their boats across the expanse of sand to where the ocean finally meets the land. With their lines dangling, Mick and Jason would wait, knowing how easily someone could find themselves trapped, caught, by the rapid turning of those tides.

As he swam in from the warm, still water to the shore, Silas, too, saw the station wagon parked out where the beach ended. He had been floating on his back, washing away the dust and grit that had clung to his skin, coating him as he had made the long walk back from Rudi's, disappointed that he had not seen Constance at all that morning. He had spent four hours trapped in the stuffiness of that shack, without once catching sight of her, listening to Rudi's enthusiastic descriptions of the latest project he had embarked upon.

It is a proving, he had explained, *a testing. The therapeutic effects of the common brown snake,* and he had shown Silas the copious notes, scrawled across scraps of paper, that he had begun to take.

You drink the venom? Silas had asked, amazed, because he had never really listened to any of Rudi's explanations; he had not even begun to understand the first elements of the process.

It is Constance who does this for me, and Rudi had spread his papers across the table. *Ideally we should have many more provers, but what can you do?* He had shrugged his shoulders.

He had wanted Silas to read his notes. He had cleared a chair for him, eagerly moving books to the floor, asking him if he was comfortable, if there was anything he could get him.

And, please, any questions, I am happy to answer.

There had been no escape. Nor had there been any possibility of just skimming the pages; Rudi had wanted to discuss it all, each point, explaining that this was only the beginning of his most important project to date. It was the differences he was looking for, the subtle differences between each of the most venomous snakes of the region, and he was relying on Constance to help him build up a picture of each potential remedy.

As Silas dried himself under the shade of a scraggly white gum, the gravel sharp beneath his feet, his whole body stiff from the hours he had spent pinned to that hard wooden chair, he wondered at how the venom had failed to harm her.

Knotting his sarong around his waist, Silas looked out to the jetty. He could see Mick waving at someone in the distance, calling out with one hand cupped around his mouth, and he turned as Steve came into view, his thick body tensed with an expectation of something about to happen as he hurried along the road towards him.

Tide's turned. He was rubbing his hands together, barely glancing in Silas's direction, as he held one thumb up, signalling to Mick that he knew, he understood and was on his way.

Out in the glaring heat of the afternoon, they gathered next to the white clock-faced tide gauge: Mick, Jason, Steve and the owner of the stranded station wagon, eager to strike a deal.

It was Steve who laid down the rules. *Beers all round, and we're talking a slab. Each.*

The owner didn't argue.

Not sure what was about to happen but curious, Silas followed, out to where the tide had risen past his calves, almost to his knees, and to where the car was rapidly sinking into the soft wet sand. This was a ritual he had not yet witnessed, and he grinned to himself as he felt the water dragging on the edge of his sarong, the weight of it, and somewhere, caught in the folds, tiny fish nibbling at the backs of his knees.

Steve told them all where to stand and Silas, who had not been given a position, took the only space available, at the driver's wheel, next to Mick.

One, two, three, easy boys. The veins stood out on Steve's face, the grunt was animal as he gave his instructions.

With both hands under the car, Silas could feel his sarong slipping away, pulled down by the water, and he wondered, for a moment, whether he should try to hold it. As he tripped on the loose cloth, he heard someone shout out, his voice a howl of pain, and then he realised he had lost it; the cloth was floating around him and he was standing there, naked to all.

It was Steve who asked him what the fuck he thought he had been doing.

It was Jason who helped Mick up to the shore.

Jesus, and as Steve lifted his sunglasses, Silas realised it was the first time he had seen him without them.

It was an accident, he protested.

Steve's spit was thick and yellow and it floated, bobbing

177

close to his calves as they made their way back to the others, the water churning around them, neither of them saying a word.

Jason already had the car, the engine at full throttle, and as Silas apologised, offering to help ease Mick into the back seat, Mick just stared at him.

It was an accident, Silas said again, and then, slightly angry now, he shook his head. *For godsakes, you don't think I did it on purpose?*

Mick just kept his eyes fixed on Silas, his gaze unwavering, as Jason slammed the door shut and Steve gunned the engine, and Silas was left standing alone, his attempt at a final protestation heard by no one but himself, the thick dust coating him as the car disappeared up the main street and headed out towards the highway.

He did not go back to Thai's until the last of the crimson in the sky had purpled and the ocean glittered black beneath the single light at the end of the jetty. He just sat there on that bench, and wondered what he was doing in this place, until finally he pulled himself up and made his way along the deserted road past the boarded-up houses and across the dirt yard.

She was on the verandah alone. The light was on in the house behind her and Silas could see Matt, back for one of his rare visits, asleep in the armchair in front of the television, the kids lying on the floor around him.

Thai just looked at him, taking a long swig of the beer by her side and wiping her mouth with the back of her hand.

Hear you pissed a few people off today, and the clink of the bottle was loud as she knocked it over, the beer spilling out in a sticky stream near her feet.

They'll get over it, Silas told her, tired now.

She stood up slowly, unsteady on her legs as she leant against the door frame, closing her eyes momentarily to stop the sickening spin in her head. She had her tobacco clutched in one hand, the dope in the other, the bottle she had just left lying in the pool of beer.

Mick reckons you've got it in for him, and she lurched slightly.

What? Silas didn't understand. He didn't even know Mick.

That's what he reckons, mate, and she coughed, trying to clear the huskiness in her throat.

Did he say why?

She just shook her head, *that's what he reckons,* the repeated words a faint mumble as she pushed the flyscreen door open and stumbled inside.

2

I was momentarily surprised when Silas told me he had been married, that he still was in fact, and then I realised it was not so out of character as I had thought.

He said he had married Rachel after knowing her for only three days. It had been a habit of his, falling in love whenever he was in an alcohol or dope-induced stupor. *Which was most of the time,* and he shook his head as he remembered. *Rachel and I were out of it from the moment we met. We thought it was a great joke. We were married in a registry and we had everyone we knew back to my place for a week-long opium-smoking binge. I didn't even remember we had got married until about a month later.* He smiled. *I had even forgotten I'd given her my grandmother's wedding ring. I woke in the middle of the night and saw it on her finger and wondered how she had ended up wearing it.*

As he spoke about Rachel, Silas recalled how he had thought he'd found perfection. He had loved the way she talked too much; he had loved the chaos that always sur-rounded her, the wild scatter of shoes, bag, matches, cigarettes, clothes that she would leave in her wake; the way she would lie back on his grandmother's chaise longue and open a bottle of wine at eleven, the ashtray overflowing next to her, and forget whatever it was she was meant to do that day; the too-dark lipstick she always wore; the pile of half-finished books she would leave on the floor; the lies she told without even blinking, her bright blue eyes steadfast as she recounted impossible stories; he had loved it all.

And I thought I loved her.

But you didn't?

I don't know. I have no idea what I thought or felt, and Silas smiled. *Sometimes I think that you can convince yourself of anything, that nothing is real.*

There is truth to what he said.

When I first slept with Greta, I did not think I loved her. Loving someone was not, for me, a prerequisite for sex. We were younger then, and when you are young, you sleep with people, and then you suddenly stop sleeping with them and you are never particularly good at articulating why you have done one or the other, nor do you think all that much about how your actions will impact on another.

So I did not think that I loved her and I didn't think, all that much, about how she felt. Despite all that, I probably whispered all the words that you whisper; I probably told her she was beautiful, I probably even made plans for what we would do, maybe hitchhiking down the coast together, perhaps a holiday overseas, I don't remember. I tried to convince myself that it was, for her as well, just sex, but later I had to admit I had been lying. I knew Greta well enough, or at least I should have known her well enough, to realise she had a fragility that should not be taken lightly.

It is still difficult for me to sort out how I felt or what she believed I felt, but I do know I would never have instigated meeting up with her again, preferring to forget rather than remember. I also know she only contacted me because of the lie Silas had told her, and that I went reluctantly, only agreeing to see her because I did not know how to say no when she suggested it, not because I had any positive desire to make amends with the past.

When she finally began to talk about what had happened all those years ago, she said that she was not sure why she had told Silas what had happened when we were together.

I hadn't told anyone before. I suppose I just felt I could. I guess I thought he was such a mess, he wouldn't judge me.

She said that she had shown him a photograph of the two of us.

From that time we went to a photo booth — you know the ones?

I didn't but I nodded.

She told me she had felt like an idiot as soon as she had brought them out for him to see, that she had grimaced as she had laid them out on the table and that Silas had laughed, that he had said it wasn't that bad, that everyone had terrible hair then.

But it wasn't that; I could see it all, right there in my face. I was such a mess.

When she had asked Silas whether he had ever behaved in a way that still made him feel sick with shame, he had not answered her.

I told him that night, she said, *I told him everything, and it was so hard to say it out loud, to recognise that person as myself.*

I looked at Greta, sitting across the table from me, and I could still only see her as she was then, over ten years ago, when I first moved into her house with her. She had advertised the bedroom at college and I was looking for somewhere to live. The room was big and cheap, and she seemed somewhat calmer at home, so I took it, and we went out for a drink to celebrate.

In those first few months, we were in that house alone. It was summer, and we would sit out in the courtyard talking, the nights hot and still, the scent of frangipani syrupy in the evening air, stray forks of lightning chasing each other across the sky as Greta told me about herself, and I listened, fascinated.

It was a car accident that had killed her mother, and she had seen it all. She had been there, in the back seat. With her knees drawn tight to her chest and her eyes wide, she would remember, bringing out new details for me each time she told the tale: the terrible thud as the car finally stopped rolling, the taste of blood in her mouth, the coldness of her mother's skin, the stupidity of the police as they tried to pull her away. I could not comprehend the enormity of the devastation she must have felt, and I would listen, astounded by her ability to speak of what seemed to me to be an immeasurably appalling tragedy.

Other nights, she would bring out photographs to show me, pictures of a beautiful woman with long honey-coloured hair. She would smile as she told me about the mud-brick house her father had built for them, and how they never wore any clothes, and how disapproving her grandparents and the rest of the town were, because it was all just too Scandinavian, too like a Swedish art-house movie. I could tell she had loved her father, before he left her, and that her mother, who had been a naturopath, was someone she still idealised, so much so that she had enrolled in a course, years later, that was so patently unsuitable for her, because she wanted to be just like her, just like her.

And then the conversation would darken, and the photographs would be put away, as she told me about her father, unable to comprehend how he could have left.

She would pour herself another wine as she said he had never even told her he was going and when she finally heard, she had made herself ill, vomiting to such an extent that she was unable to leave her bedroom and the coolness of the flannel her grandmother put on her forehead.

She lit another cigarette as she recounted receiving the news of his second marriage, and how she had jumped off the roof of the barn, only to succeed in breaking her leg.

It wasn't the first time I'd tried, she said.

And as the thunder cracked across the sky, and the first rain began to fall, I tucked her long blonde hair behind her ears and I kissed her.

You know I lost my virginity when I was fourteen, she whispered. *To the local doctor.*

I didn't.

I've had four terminations, she added.

And I just kissed her again, never really listening to the truth behind all she was saying, never really thinking about who she was, never really seeing all that she was trying to reveal.

The first time we slept together we were so stoned the room seemed to float around us. That much I do remember. The second time, I was surprised. I had thought it was just one of those things that probably wouldn't be repeated. The third time, she told me she loved me and I laughed; *you don't know me,* I said.

And she told me she did.

Sometimes, thinking I was asleep, she would lie leaning on her elbow and look at me. When I caught her, she would turn away, embarrassed.

Sometimes she would ask me why I was with her, if it was a mistake I regretted, and I would swear that it wasn't.

I remember the extent of her need when we made love, and the extent of her withdrawal when I was not interested.

I'm too tired, I would tell her, and she would turn her back to me and not speak for hours.

I remember the extravagance of the gift she gave me when we had been together for a month -- a collection of texts that I knew had cost her far more than she could afford.

I remember the slight unease I felt as she clung to my arm when we were out together, kissing me passionately in front of others, claiming me as her own, sullen and unwilling to communicate if I did not give her all of my attention.

I remember the times she listened in to my phone conversations, the times I caught her searching through my letters, the tears and apologies, and the terrible feeling that I had become involved in something I was unable to end.

You have never loved me, she would say and I would usually end up lying, thinking that somehow this would all work itself out, she'd had countless lovers, she would move onto someone else, it would be all right.

Had I been older and wiser I would have attempted to extricate myself much earlier than I did, I would have realised that need does not equal love. But that's not the way it was. In any event, the brief time of living by ourselves came to an end when Victoria arrived, and I suppose I thought it would change with someone else in the house.

Victoria was Greta's best friend from high school. She had been travelling in Europe and when Greta had heard she was coming back, she had promised to save the other room for her. I came down one morning to find her there, in the kitchen, home a week early, and I remember thinking 'Thank God', because I was, by then, in a permanent state of anxiety. I had to end it, I knew that, I just didn't want to leave her alone, and I didn't want to have to deal with the consequences, not by myself. 'Victoria will help', I thought, 'Victoria will help', and I smiled as I told her who I was; *Daniel,* I said, and she grinned as she kissed me, once on each cheek; *Victoria,* she told me, and I said that I knew, that I'd heard all about her, that I was pleased she was back. *Really?* she asked, one eyebrow raised; *really,* I smiled.

When I saw Greta again, I was afraid she would ask me whether I had ever loved her, but she didn't. Nor did she ask whether there was any truth to all she had accused me of; her references to our past were far briefer and more honest than I had expected.

She told me that she shouldn't have tried to hurt me in the way that she did, that I had always been kind to her, that was what she remembered, and as she looked straight at me, I felt only shame at my own dishonesty, but still I did not speak, still I did nothing to ease some of the guilt she felt, and when she reached for my hand, I pulled away, scratching my arm, pretending I was unaware of her gesture.

— 3 —

Silas told me that once he had started the task, this division of who he was into different categories, he found it difficult to stop. The piles began to spread out across his grandmother's Persian carpets, placed to map out the links that lay between each person he had been. When he finally finished, he counted 227 in all.

I was amazed, he said, *at how fractured one life could be.*

Kneeling on the floor, Silas looked again at the divisions he had created; all the aspects of who he was before he went to Port Tremaine. As he began to gather the papers, uncertain as to what he would do with them, he realised he had nothing to mark who he was now.

He stopped for a moment, a few sheets clutched in his hand, the latest scars on his arms right before his eyes.

In his bedroom he found the notes on Kirlian photography that he had made in the library, the countless attempts at a letter to Rudi, the lists he had written, and he gathered them up, placing them neatly in the centre of the maze. This was where it had all led to, he thought. This was what he had become, and he looked at it, complete now, before gathering it up, all of it put in boxes out in the hall-way, ready to be burnt.

— 4 —

If it had not been for Constance, the accident with Mick would have marked the time for Silas's departure. Whatever party there had been was now well and truly over, and he knew it. The place he had found for himself, there on the verandah with Thai and the others, was gone. He had been tolerated because, once again, he had supplied the drugs and alcohol. He knew that was how it was, he had never held any doubts about it, because that was how he had always found his way through life, purchasing a brief time of comparative ease that he could enter and leave as he pleased.

But in the days that followed the accident, Silas knew Mick's broken foot had changed his status in the town. The next morning, after Matt drove off into the first fierce rays of the sun stretching across the flatness of the land, after the low throb of Steve's car signalled his return to his place on the verandah, Silas left for the garden as he always did, but this time there was no nod in his direction as he passed, no joint held out for him. The snigger of the kids as he crossed the dirt yard let him know how far the story of the previous day's 'fiasco' (as Pearl had taken to calling it) had travelled, but it did not matter. Constance was his only concern; all he wanted was for her to see him, to recognise how he felt and to perhaps even like him in return.

I guess that was what I always did, he told me. *When one thing died, I threw myself headlong into the next. I was already heading that way, I was already making her into my single obsession.*

And after the accident, he just took it that little bit further.

How do you do it? he asked her, pleased to have once again found that it was her, not Rudi, who had come to let him in as he had pressed himself against the gate and called out her name.

Do what? She had the keys in her hand and she shook them, the metal sparkling in the brightness of the sun as she pointed at the gate. *Open this?*

He was hot. The sweat was sticky on his forehead and he could smell the staleness of the alcohol he had drunk alone in his room the previous night, there on his skin, overpowering even the sweetness of her. When he had crashed out on the hardness of the floor, the bottle empty, it was snakes that he had dreamt about, thousands of them coiling, slippery smooth, the coldness of their flesh pressed against his own.

Or is it drinking venom that you are referring to? She unlocked the padlock and let him in, her smile amused.

He felt the coolness of the garden as soon as he stepped

inside and he wondered at how she had once again been aware of his thoughts. *I could try too,* he offered, grinning at the idea. *You need others. I could help.*

She stepped back. *I think you are poisoned enough as it is,* and she waved her hand across her face, wrinkling her nose slightly at the sourness of his skin.

I'm serious, he told her, because the notion did entice him; the thought of entering their world was both exciting and, he had to admit, a little frightening. *Why not? I could join you out here. There used to be others.*

She was amused now. *How long would you last?*

I don't know, and he didn't. He looked at her smiling at him, her arms folded across her chest, her eyes glittering in the sharpness of the light. *Oh, you are so beautiful.* The words were out before he even thought to stop them. What did it matter? *You have no idea,* he was holding her hands now, trying to dance with her, to swing her round under the strange rush of the branches overhead, the cool sway of green, the gentleness of the breeze, all of it moving, none of it still. *We could start it up again, just the three of us, and then there would be others, and who knows how far it would go. Why not? Why not?*

Don't. It was all she said.

And I could read to you, at night, because he remembered how she had once told him that there had been a young woman who used to tell her stories before she went to sleep, and another who had taught her songs, nursery songs that she could still recall, all from the time before, the early years when it had not been just her and Rudi, alone.

Please. Her eyes narrowed and her smile was close to a grimace.

It would not have been enough to stop him; he would have continued regardless, if he had not happened in that instant to see Rudi, right there on the path behind her, one hand raised in greeting, the other clutching what appeared to be a bird, its body limp in his grasp. At the sound of his footsteps, she moved back.

He is not well, she whispered.

Rudi looked pale. Silas could only presume he had been drinking again, but he knew better than to refer to Rudi's occasional binges – he had seen Constance's anger the few times he had come close to touching on the matter, he had experienced her sharp dismissals; *you have no idea,* she would say, *you have no right to judge.*

I meant it, he urged her now. *Just think about it,* he whispered.

She nodded but she had already turned away, she was already calling out to her father.

We have lunch, he told her, holding out what Silas could now see was a duck, the brilliant green of its feathers slicked flat against its still body.

Silas just looked in horror at the dead animal. *You killed it?* His agitation at what had failed to pass with Constance made him more appalled than he would otherwise have been.

Rudi smiled. *Of course. If we are to eat flesh, we must take life. It can be no other way.*

But Silas was not listening.

In that brief moment, she had gone again, disappeared into the thick tangle of colour, the path between the flowers seeming to close behind her so that all he saw was the crisp blue of the man's shirt she always wore, and then nothing.

Wait, he called after her, the promise he had attempted to extract from her now floating around him, his whole body tensed with the frustration of having been so close, but only for a moment.

Come, Rudi's grasp was firm. *She has work to do, and so do we.*

— 5 —

Samantha, another supervisor, has told Jeanie that she is a little concerned about one of her provers.

It is Megan, Jeanie explained to me. *Apparently she has a crush on you.*

Me? I was surprised, and somewhat confused.

I do not even know her. We had gone walking together in one of the gorges once, and she had told me about the novel she had been trying to write. I must admit, I barely listened. I had wanted to be on my own, but when she had asked if she could join me, I had thought it would have been rude to refuse. Apart from that, I have spent no time with her.

I began to apologise, but Jeanie stopped me.

It's not your fault, she assured me. *Apparently Megan is like that. Samantha was unsure as to whether she'd be suitable, but decided to give her a go. She just doesn't know whether she should continue, whether it will affect her findings.*

There are definite characteristics one needs in a prover: good health is one, attention to detail is another, and a certain level of emotional stability is another.

Maybe if I talked to her? I offered, hearing the reluctance in my own voice. I did not want this. I did not know what I was expected to do about it.

No, no, Jeanie rushed to explain, *I only wanted to discuss whether she should continue.*

I told her I didn't feel I should be the one giving an opinion on the matter; I did not know why, but I felt uncomfortable.

Samantha knows her, I said. *Besides, an attraction doesn't necessarily go hand in hand with emotional instability.*

Jeanie smiled. *I know,* and she apologised again for having brought it up with me.

Tonight as we ate dinner together, I sat at the other end of the table from Megan and wished I had never been told. She has decided that she will go, and she has spoken to everyone except me. If I am honest, I have had moments of wondering why she was selected. When we went for a walk together, I was struck by her eagerness to be liked, by her nervousness. But perhaps I am overly sensitive to such character traits, perhaps I judge her in retrospect.

I remember the letters Greta sent me after she was taken to hospital. She blamed all that had happened on love (her excessive love for me and my lack of love for her) rather than her own precarious sense of place within the world. At least, in the ones I read, she did. She sent them to my father's house, and he would bring them round to where

I was living with Victoria. Eventually, I told him not to. I could not read them.

Why? he asked me.

Because I was the one who found her. I was the one who came home and called out her name. I was the one who got no answer. I was the one who opened the bedroom door to see her lying there, grey and limp, eyes blank; I was the one who shook her, trying to wake her, over and over again.

My father understood. He had, after all, found my mother once, years earlier, in a similar state.

I called the ambulance. I can still remember my inability to dial the number, uncertain as to whether it was triple 0 or triple 9 I should be trying. I can still remember vomiting, the cold fear remaining in my stomach as I washed my face. I can still remember begging her to wake up as I waited, for what seemed to be an interminable time, for them to arrive.

That was the way she had known it would be. That was what she had wanted.

I did not go with Greta into casualty and I was not with her when she had her stomach pumped. I did not visit her afterwards and I did not answer any of her letters. I could not see her. I could not open it all up again.

Eventually, she, too, stopped trying.

When we met again, she told me that after she had been discharged, she had gone back to her grandparents' farm for a few months. I knew that already. I had seen the postmarks on all the envelopes my father had given to me. Eventually she had moved to another city. She had studied art for five years and then she had come back.

You know, she said, *I can understand why you didn't want to see me. I even understood it then,* she grimaced slightly, hating the memory of what she had been like, *but I never understood Victoria.* She looked away. *She was my best friend.*

And still I didn't say a word.

— 6 —

I do not know whether Greta asked Silas to try a little harder, whether she urged him to attempt to talk to me again, but when he arrived for our next appointment, I sensed a greater desire in him to speak the truth.

He was tense when he sat down, his entire body rigid as he braced himself for what he knew was bound to follow, and his answers were, at first, monosyllabic to even the most innocuous of questions.

We spent the first part of the appointment talking about the isolation of his life, and he soon tired of it. He felt we were simply going around in circles.

I was always someone who just went along with whatever was happening, he explained. *I never made any attempts to assert an identity. Even my rebellions, for what they were worth, were no more than what you would expect a bored rich kid to do. I was easygoing, so people hung around. And there was also my money.*

I asked him whether he had ever considered the possibility he might have been liked by some of the people he had met. He did not respond.

And now? I sat back.

Silas looked at the ceiling without blinking. *I've removed myself. It's just the way it has to be.*

I had chosen more regular follow-up visits than I would normally schedule because I had felt a concern, a need to closely monitor his progress, but I had delayed prescribing further treatment. I had wanted to assess the effect of the initial remedy over a period of time before I considered whether I should select another. When I told him this, adding that I am not always orthodox in my approach, that I sometimes choose a more dynamic intervention, he finally smiled.

He said that the initial remedy I gave him had not appeared particularly dynamic. The drops had simply tasted like sugar. He had felt no radical impact, although he did have to admit there had been an undeniable lessening in his heart pains, and he looked surprised, as though the realisation had not occurred until that moment.

We could probably go on using it, I said. *In fact, everything you have told me would seem to indicate that it is more than appropriate. But,* and I smiled at him, *I'm always open to stirring things up. A shake-up can sometimes work wonders.*

Silas shrugged. *Whatever,* and he pulled at the hem of his sleeve, trying to cover the fresh sores puncturing his flesh.

I told him we needed to go back to what we had begun to discuss at the last appointment and I saw him scratch at his ankle, crossing and uncrossing his legs as though he could not find a comfortable position in which to sit.

The most recent episode, it was last night? I glanced quickly at the notes I had made and Silas nodded.

Did you see anything? Hear anything?

He had already told me that he had not been surprised to find himself awake at four in the morning, inspecting the fresh wounds under the light of his bedside lamp. He had come home at midnight, agitated, anxious about sleeping.

I had been out, drinking with Greta, he had explained. *It was the alcohol, I suppose. It made me think I could ask her home, it made me forget what I do to myself. But she was in a strange mood. She had told me stuff. About herself,* and he had looked away, his face betraying the discomfort he had suddenly felt in discussing her with me. *So we parted.*

He had still not told me whether he had experienced any sensations prior to waking, and he knew it. He swallowed, his mouth dry as he finally attempted to answer my question.

I guess I've been lying.

In the stillness I could hear the clock in reception click over and, from the other end of the building, the soft thud of the heavy doors that lead onto the street. This was the time when we closed them. People who were booked in for after-hours appointments were instructed to ring the buzzer. Fortunately, I had made no additional appointments for the day, knowing Silas was last on my list and that we would need time.

His voice was tight as he attempted to explain. *When I told you that I don't know, that was when I was lying.*

Know what?

What I am doing to myself.

It was the sweetness, the rich headiness of Constance's flowers that he always smelt, somewhere in his subconscious. As he tried to describe it, I saw a trickle of sweat running down the back of his neck, and I watched as he wiped at it, agitated.

So, you see, I am not entirely unaware.

I nodded.

And the thing is, I can stop it, at that stage, I can wake myself up. I don't have to do this, he held out his arm. *It's a choice.*

And you choose this?

He looked at the ground.

Why?

He shifted in his chair. *Because I want to.* He pushed his sleeves up and stared at the wounds.

I did not speak for a moment. I was hoping he would continue, and I watched him as he struggled for an explanation. He bit his lip, the flesh white beneath his teeth. He scratched at his wrist. He closed his eyes. Finally, I leant a little closer.

And do you see anything? When you are hurting yourself?

He was about to shake his head, but then he stopped. There was no point in further lies. Staring out the window, he finally answered my question, and for a moment I did not understand.

Myself.

I looked at him. *Are you watching yourself hurting yourself?*

Silas shook his head.

Are you doing anything?

No. I just see my own face.

I waited.

Silas's intake of breath was sharp. *It is hatred.*

I opened my mouth to speak but I did not know what to say. We looked at each other in silence for what was only an instant, a missed beat, but felt longer. I remember that I wanted to touch him, I wanted to reach out and hold his arm in my hand, wrapping my own fingers around the wide open sores, but I knew that if I moved, he would only pull away. I could see it on his face. All that he wanted was to go. He could see no point in any of this; there was nothing I could do. With his hands pressed down on the arm of the chair, he attempted to stand, and that was when I moved, laying my fingers across his elbow.

So, what is it this time? Silas's voice was tired. *Another spider?*

I shook my head.

A snake? As he uttered the words, I wondered at the disgust in his voice.

I smiled. *No.* I tore the page off my notebook. *This,* and I pointed to Silas's arm, *is not a snake.*

Silas looked at me.

I needed my voice to be gentle. *A snake is too self-possessed to act in this way.* I held out the page for him to take. *I'd like to try Belladonna this time.*

Silas sighed. *It can't change what I did. Nothing can — poison, venom, plant, animal, what does it matter?*

I didn't understand.

I didn't act quickly enough. I saw she had been bitten and I didn't know what to do. I went to get help, but it was too late.

It still made no sense. What he had done was not so bad.

And that's all? I asked, unable to hide the confusion in my voice.

He did not reply. He was tapping his fingers on his knees, drumming them, trying to distract himself from the sudden desire he had to weep, because he knew how close we had come; we were standing right at the brink of the hole that was himself and he could not bear it.

There was more to his story, that much was clear. Later, I would wonder at my inability to see what was obvious, but at that stage I simply wanted him to understand that we were not seeking to change the past. No one can do that.

It is a question of being able to make peace.

He looked at me.

Being in a position to do that.

That's what I would like, and although his expression was one of doubt, it was as though he had suddenly realised he had been searching for the wrong goal.

I watched him, the awareness flickering across his face, and as we stared at each other, I let the pain go, because it was only in that instant that I realised I had been holding it in my own flesh, the hard hatred of the wounds I had been touching, there in my own body, and I breathed in, slowly and deeply, desperately needing the sweetness of the air fresh in my lungs.

— 7 —

The night after Silas attempted to tell Constance that he loved her, he came back to Thai's to find them all on the verandah: Steve, Jason and Mick. Not one of them looked in his direction as he passed. In his room, his belongings had been pulled out of his bag and hastily repacked. He had not bothered to hide the little cash he kept on him. It was there, next to his bed, underneath a pile of papers, but whoever had searched through his room had missed it.

He sat on the floor, the dry, bare boards creaking beneath his weight, a single fly buzzing loudly near his head. From outside, he could hear the shattering of glass as Steve threw another empty bottle onto the pile. Silas put his head in his hands, the dirt caked into every crevice of his skin, and closed his eyes. Tonight he would pack. Tomorrow he would tell Constance that if there was no place for him out there with her, he would go.

He had sat through lunch, trying to eat the roast duck Rudi had served, the fat congealing on the enamel plates, the meat sinking heavy and indigestible to the pit of his stomach. He was aware only of her opposite him, and the realisation that he had meant what he said, he wanted to be with her, he needed to be with her.

It was Rudi who had done all the talking.

Everything you eat, all of it, he had told Silas several times, *has no poison, no chemicals. See how good it is,* and he had smacked his lips in pleasure at the taste. *Look at my daughter, this is what she eats; see her skin, her eyes,* and his own eyes had softened as he had looked across at Constance. *This is good health. This is how it should be. But do they listen?* and he had nodded in the direction of Port Tremaine as he had repeated his old refrain. *Not a word. And then they wonder what is happening to their country, their town.*

Silas had looked across at Constance but her attention was, invariably, directed elsewhere. It was shyness, that was all it was. He had said too much. He had scared her. She would have had no experience with men. He had to be more careful, more gentle. This was what he kept telling himself in an attempt to convince himself that the truth was as he would have liked it to be.

He had watched as she'd cleared the plates, amazed at the ease with which she had moved around the shack, without any apparent need to feel her way past obstacles. Sometimes the veracity of Rudi's claims concerning her vision seemed undeniable, and as he had stood up to help her, he found himself staring at her. It was then that Rudi had doubled over for one brief moment (*Indigestion,* he had tried to explain a few seconds later), and she had turned to him in alarm, despite the fact that he had not uttered a sound.

It is nothing, Rudi had insisted, and she had not taken her eyes from him, seeming to assess something not visible to anyone in the room but her.

There had been no opportunity to talk to her after lunch.

We have work to do, she had told him.

It was Rudi who had urged him to stay, and he had done so despite Constance's apparent discomfort at the idea.

In the still heat of that one room, they had sat around the table, Constance talking and Rudi taking down her every word, his writing scrawling across the scraps of paper he used as he had recorded her responses to his questions, leaning forward eagerly, nodding in excitement as she had attempted to tell him how each aspect of her physical, emotional and mental being had responded to the remedy they were proving.

Watching them, Silas had been aware that his presence was no longer even noticed by either of them. Witnessing the intensity of their communication, he had been drawn into the strength of their belief, the importance of each detail as Rudi had probed further: what was it exactly, that slight ache in her left temple as the sun went down; the dream she'd had of flying; the aversion towards the afternoon winds that swept up from the gulf; could she describe it further, with more detail, and she had tried over and over again.

We must be painstaking, Rudi had once explained to him. *We must record everything, no matter how small, how unimportant, before we can even begin to see the total picture. What is this venom, that is what I am asking. What is it?*

That evening as he lay in his room out the back of Thai's, a bottle of vodka on the floor next to his bed, Silas closed his eyes and tried to see her. She had sat facing her father, still and calm, and she had given him everything he had wanted, each intimate detail, believing, as Rudi did, in the importance of what they were trying to achieve.

He has done extraordinary work, she had told Silas once. *If you listened to him, you would know.*

But I do listen, Silas had protested, uncomfortable in the face of her disbelief.

Before the others left, there were enough of us; people took note of our results.

Why did you stay? Silas had asked her and she had shrugged as though his question barely warranted an answer.

He does not keep me here, and she had pointed to the keys in her pocket. *He is my father,* and she had shaken her head in wonder at his stupidity.

Watching the pair of them after lunch, Silas had seen the care she had given to each of her responses, until, as Rudi had come close to the end of his questions, she had pulled back.

She had known what Rudi's request was before he had even spoken it out loud; his whole body had been bent towards her, his large hands outstretched. There was no point, she had said. *How can I?* and she had folded her hands in her lap.

It was what she saw, that was what he wanted to know; a tiny glass bottle containing the venom clutched in one hand, he had begged her to tell him. *What is it?* he had pleaded, all of him believing that if she could just paint him a picture of what it was that danced before her eyes, he would know, he would be able to see.

Knocking over the vodka, the last drops spilling across the floor of his room, Silas searched for his phone among the mess of clothes littered across the top of his bag. He tried each of the numbers that he could somehow still remember, grinning to himself at the ludicrousness of being able to hear friends' voices disembodied on answering machines, hanging up each time the message came to an end. He even attempted to ring his mother, forgetting for a moment that she had died, wishing that he could speak to someone, any-one, and then suddenly, to her in particular, only realising that this was impossible when he heard the operator's recorded voice tell him the call could not be connected.

The last number he tried was Sarah Lipscombe's. She had been Rachel's best friend, until Silas had slept with her. He was surprised when she answered, and when she asked him what he had been doing, he did not know what to say. Sitting with his back against the rusted iron bed, he closed his eyes to the dim light of the single bulb overhead and tried to describe Constance and the garden.

She's unbelievable, he said, hearing the slur in his voice, and he opened his eyes briefly to the slow sickening spin of the room. *A witch – tames snakes, sees auras, heals with plants.*

He knew that his words had failed to paint Constance in the manner in which he wanted and he tried to stand, slowly pulling himself up on the chenille bedspread, only to crash to the floor with the effort.

Are you all right? Sarah asked.

Silas laughed.

You're drunk, she said.

Silas didn't deny it.

It's bloody weird here, he told her, and he was suddenly overwhelmed by a desire to go home, knowing that he was spinning now, untethered and out of control.

He heard her sigh. *Maybe you should call when you're sober.*

I guess, and Silas looked out the window at the night sky, a spread of stars too numerous to count.

I don't know why I hoped you'd get it together while you were away. Her tone turned to one of irritation. *Why do you waste your life?* And she was silent for a moment. *Forget it. It's none of my business.*

As Silas let the phone fall to the ground and lay back on

the floor, the sound of Thai and Steve's fucking carrying through the heat of the night air, it was Rudi he saw; the desperation in his eyes as Constance had told him he was asking for the impossible, a description of something he would never be able to see. She had turned to the window, her expression unreadable.

Besides, she had muttered, her voice barely above a whisper, *it's mine.*

And Silas had watched as she had wiped at the tears with the back of her hand.

the direction of cure

Cure proceeds from above downward, from within outward, from the most important organs to the least important organs, and in the reverse order of appearance of symptoms.

Constantine Hering (1800–1880)

~ 1 ~

There is a thick white mist this morning, dense enough to obscure all vision from the small window next to my bed. I sleep on the mezzanine, and when I wake it is always the sky that greets me first, just the sky.

I lie here, knowing the others are still asleep, and as I close my eyes again, it is the track that I see, the path that Silas described for me, a spidery trail of yellow dirt pockmarked with sharp stones, weaving through the low-lying scrub that stretches between the town and Rudi's.

Silas told me that when the idea of returning first came to him, shortly after he commenced taking Belladonna, it was that trail he saw. In the days that followed, he would picture himself, standing where the road petered out into dust, the last house on his right, the paleness of the gulf waters on his left, the thick brush, steel grey, in front of him, and through it, the track he had worn.

The trail he had made had, of course, long since gone by the time I got to Port Tremaine. Pearl attempted to explain how I would find my way out there, but it was Steve who drew me the map, any hostility he might have felt towards Silas and those who knew him quickly overcome by a more powerful desire to talk.

His kids rode their rusted trikes over the drawing he had scratched into the dirt as soon as he finished it.

Twins, he told me proudly, and I noticed that they were, indeed, alike.

He drew the map again, grinning as he wiped over what remained of his previous attempt.

You know there's nothing there now? He looked at me quizzically as I tried to explain that it didn't matter. I just wanted to see it for myself, to picture what it had once been.

Steve also told me where Mick had gone. I had seen the closed garage, boarded up, the sign advertising repairs barely legible now, the rust corroding the black painted letters so that they bled into the yellow background.

Poor bastard, and he ran his fingers through the thick wiry hair of one of the boys, now clinging to his jeans. *Should have told us,* he shook his head. *But you know how it is. Still waters.* He picked the other child up, taking a last swig from the stubbie in his free hand.

Shel. His voice was loud, and I saw the woman, heavily pregnant, come to the door of the house behind us. *Get us another, would you, darl?* He held the empty bottle up, and the flyscreen slammed shut behind her.

Mick had not spoken to any of them, not until

afterwards. When Steve told me where he had gone, I thought about driving to the town on the other side of the gulf and attempting to talk to him but there really wasn't any point. I already knew what little there was to know.

It was not until the night before Mick left that he finally revealed it all to Steve. The pair of them had sat out on the end of the jetty, chucking their empty bottles into the swollen evening tide, and he had cried.

Like a baby, and Steve had shaken his head in wonder. *He didn't get there until a month after it happened. Couldn't walk, couldn't drive. His foot was broken. When he finally made it out there, the old bloke was drunk. Said he'd buried her himself. Had no idea why Mick would care. Why Mick wanted to know.*

As I lie in my bed and remember Steve's words, I open my eyes again to find that the mist has begun to thin into tufts of grey cottonwool pulled across the blankness of the sky. I should get up. I should not stay here, steeped in the desolation of that town. I can hear the others waking in the rooms below me and I test the chill in the air, pushing my blanket down a little. I will light the fire.

In a couple of days, the provers will commence taking the remedies and we have planned a breakfast meeting today to answer any last questions about the process.

We agreed on the meeting because there have been rumblings of concern about the lasting effects of an experience such as the one we are about to embark on. Just the other day, Matthew asked me whether the remedy could have a long-term detrimental effect on his health. He posed the question casually, but I could see it was a serious worry.

I told him it was highly unlikely. The risk of experiencing minor suffering during the process was more possible, and I smiled as I added that this wasn't necessarily negative. Poets, writers, musicians and artists would all testify to the benefits of suffering.

And we are really only talking about minor discomfort here.

But I didn't want him to think that I was simply dismissing his concerns. Even if a long-term detrimental effect is unlikely, it is still a possibility, and neither he nor I (nor any of the others) should take this process lightly.

Everything that we do, everything that we experience, adds to the picture of who we are. It is retained within us. They were words I had once spoken to Silas and I repeated them to Matthew.

We were unpacking the boxes as we talked, checking the labelling on the bottles to ensure they matched up with the provers and supervisors who are here. He held one up for a moment, turning the glass in his hand, and I must admit that, for the first time, I was curious.

I wonder what it is, I said, almost to myself, and he grinned at me.

I smiled back as I told him that I am, after all, only human.

He looked at the bottle and then put it down. *It's amazing, isn't it?*

I did not know what he meant, not at first.

That whatever it is has gone, has been diluted so much that it doesn't exist.

It still exists, I said, knowing I was being pedantic, because I did understand him.

You once told me that it is like there is just a memory.

I knew the explanation I had given him because I have given it to many of my patients. Think of the water as having a memory, I would say, of retaining all the necessary information about the substance that has been passed through it; and I would see them attempting to come to terms with the idea.

As I get up, the chill worse than I had anticipated, I think about how the power of this memory still amazes me. Each time I see it at work, I bow my head to its force, because it is far stronger than any matter, any substance, and its effects are extraordinary to witness.

2

I don't know what made Silas lie to me when he told me that Greta wanted to talk to me. Perhaps he just felt that getting us together again would be positive, beneficial for at least one of us, perhaps even both of us.

At that stage, I did not even know that Greta had told him the story of our relationship. I must admit to an initial irritation when she confessed to having spoken to him about us. She knew he was my patient and it seemed to me to be an irresponsible act, an invasion. A few moments later I realised I was probably overreacting. I was too sensitive to a patient being privy to my personal life, too quick to infer that if I was seen as human I would not be as effective in my treatment. Probably the reverse is true. I don't really know.

I was driving Silas home at the time he gave me her supposed message. I had found him at the bus stop after our appointment, his long legs stretched out in front of him, his eyes fixed on the pavement. I almost didn't disturb him, he seemed to be absorbed in thought, but then I remembered there was a transport strike called for the early evening, a fact that I knew would have escaped him.

He was careful in his conversation. This is the way it often is with patients when you see them after hours. They are wary of imposing; Silas particularly so. We talked about our weekends. He told me he had no plans and I had to admit to the same. I had been asked out to dinner by one of Victoria's friends but I did not know if I was up to hearing news of her.

When we pulled up outside his apartment block, he said that Greta had asked him to say hello.

I knew I had failed to hide the surprise on my face, and I pretended to search for money in the loose change I kept in the ashtray.

She asked me to give you her number. To say that she'd like to catch up, and he handed me a slip of paper.

As soon as he closed the door, I let it fall to the ground, losing it in the pile of rubbish and papers that always clutters the floor of my car.

Later, Greta told me she had done no such thing.

She also said that only moments after she had told Silas what she had done when we were together, she wished she had kept silent. Silas had walked her home. Standing outside her door, she had told him it was a pathetic story and one that she would rather he forget.

It's not so bad, and he had reached for her hand but she had pulled away. *Trust me,* he had said, *I know.*

But she had felt ashamed. Unable to look at herself in the mirror, she had wondered how he would see her now. Switching off her light and getting into bed, she had told herself it would be best if she just kept away for a while. She did not have to go to the library anymore. She could finish off her work from home, and as she had closed her eyes, she had hated the importance of the place he had assumed in her life and how difficult it was for her, still, to allow closeness without fear.

— *3* —

Why do you wear a skirt?

Lucas was sitting on the floor of Silas's room, pushing his Matchbox car across the rotting boards, carefully negotiating the rugged terrain. It was not even nine o'clock and already the heat was unbearable. The tiny window next to Silas's bed provided the only ventilation in a house that baked under a tin roof, and it only opened three inches.

Most mornings Silas woke with a hangover, but this was the worst. He had told Lucas to leave him alone, but he had only backed a little closer to the door, and Silas could still hear the whine of Lucas's attempts to sound like a car, punctuated by his insistent questioning.

Are you a poof? Lucas asked, clearly uncertain as to what the word meant.

Silas rinsed his face over the sink. The water was tepid, and he could see Lucas in the mirror, still talking.

Jason reckons you are.

It was drinking alone that was the problem. He had no outside check on how much he had consumed. But the truth was, even if he had been able to find someone who would have been willing to keep him company, he would probably still have chosen to be by himself. He was going under and he knew it.

Martha reckons you must have been in some kind of funny business to come out here. She reckons you're in hiding, and Lucas revved his car a little harder in an attempt to get it across a cracked board near the door. *Steve just reckons you're a wanker.*

Silas needed Panadol. As he fumbled through his bag, knowing he would be unlikely to find anything, he glanced across at Lucas. The boy's freckled face was upturned, his blue eyes were watery with what looked to be conjunctivitis, and he was staring straight back at Silas.

No one seems to like you much anymore.

Silas just turned and vomited once again, a dry retch that ripped at his throat, and made the pounding in his head even stronger.

Wiping his mouth, he pushed his way past Lucas and stumbled out into the burning heat of the morning, the boy's voice thin and high as he called out a couple of times and then, realising it was useless, gave up and turned back inside.

There was no Panadol at Pearl's, only Aspro and Bex, the cardboard boxes faded, the use-by stamps illegible. Silas picked up the least ancient-looking packet and, not being in any mood for conversation, waited for her to name the price.

She told him he looked like something the cat had

dragged in. She was chewing a caramel as she spoke. Silas could see it rolling around inside her mouth, caught momentarily in a gap between her teeth and then loosened again by the force of her suck.

Hear Mick won't be walking for a while, and a gob of sweet sticky spit landed on the edge of the Aspro box. *Guess that leaves the playing field to you.*

Silas had no idea what she meant. He counted out what he could only presume to be close to adequate payment and pushed the money towards her.

Hmph, and she crossed her arms, pressing them tight against the strain of cloth across her bosom. *That'll be another five.*

Silas added a five-cent piece to the pile.

Dollars.

He was made of money and they knew it, each and every one of them. It was, in fact, the only thing he was good for, his only worth in a place like this.

Look at them, and the sharpness of his tone revealed his anger as he wiped the layer of brown dirt off the box.

Pearl just unwrapped another caramel and popped it in her mouth, her tongue tracing the flaking edges of her pink lipstick, as she deposited the money into her cashbox and then held out her hand for the expected note.

Haven't been so sociable lately, and she peered at him through her thick glasses.

It was true, he hadn't been visiting her as frequently.

Hear you're up there every day of the week now. She nodded in the direction of Rudi's. *From the looks of you this morning, it hasn't been doing you any good.*

Silas ignored her comment.

Pearl just shook her head. *You're looking as bad as he does.*

Silas could only presume she was talking about Rudi.

Drinks himself into a stupor on a regular basis. She sniffed in disapproval. *It'll be the death of him. Not that he'd be missed around here.*

Well, she'd miss him, Silas told her, suddenly aware of how impossible Constance's situation would be without her father.

Pearl sucked hard on her sweet. *She'll be all right.* Her eyes were sharp. *Seems to me she has no problems getting men to run around after her.*

Out in the stillness of the morning, the heat already ferocious, Silas looked up and down the empty street and wanted only to be out of there. He hated this town. He brushed his hand across his face, disturbing the flies that gathered the instant he was still, three or four of them circling slowly, waiting only for another opportunity to alight. He tilted his head back and swallowed an aspirin, the glare from the sun blinding him for a moment, the tablet getting stuck in the back of his throat, so that he was forced to cough, a sour powdery taste remaining in his mouth as he swallowed.

It had been three days since he had seen Constance. *Where is she?* he had kept asking Rudi, barely able to contain his agitation now, not sure why they all still persisted in carrying out this charade of pretending it was Rudi he wanted to see. She had made him promise he would be kind to her father, and he had tried, but he could no longer sit in that shack, the closed heat thick with the rankness of Rudi's breath and the sweat on his skin. Standing by the window, the overblown sweetness of the flowers making his head reel, he would ask Rudi if he knew when she would be back, would it be soon, his questions always remaining unanswered, barely heard in fact. He would tap his feet, fidget, scratch at his arms, knowing that all he could do was look for her, and hope that she would appear, a dream-like vision, surrounded by blooms that seemed too intense, too surreal, too luminous and brilliant.

Turning towards the end of the road, to the sandy track that would take him back out to Constance, Silas told himself it would be different this time. It had to be. He walked more quickly, oblivious to the heat, the flies and the scrub, seeing only the glittering beauty of the garden, not far now, and with both hands on the gate, he called out their names, *Rudi, Constance*, surprised that no one came to let him in, that Rudi was not nearby, waiting anxiously for his arrival.

He pulled himself up on the cyclone fencing, and as he swung his legs over the vicious twists of wire along the top, he did not even notice that one of them had ripped through his jeans, gouging into his flesh. He was worried now, and he called out her name again, *Constance*, finally catching a glimpse of her shirt, there in the distance, as he dropped to the ground.

She was alone. Silas could not believe his luck, and as he ran towards her, there by the rainwater tank just outside the shack, he was unaware that Rudi was lying inside, unable to move.

~ 4 ~

When Greta apologised to me, she told me that all she could say in her own defence was that she felt she had descended to a type of madness.

I look back on the way I behaved, and I do not understand it. It was like standing at the top of a muddy slope and slipping down, trying to hold on, but being unable to find anything to grasp.

She said she knew there had been no rational basis to all her fears, and she glanced across at me, her need for affirmation still there, revealed for a brief moment only, and then hidden again, far more effectively than she had ever been able to do when I used to know her.

I should have just trusted that you loved me, but once I began doubting it, I couldn't stop.

She apologised for all the times she had searched through my belongings, for all the accusations she had made, for all the hysterical rages and threats and, finally, for believing that I was sleeping with Victoria.

That was the most unfair, and she looked out across the street.

She was silent for a moment, breathing in sharply before she spoke again.

When I did what I did, her discomfort made her fidget more anxiously with her hair, her voice cracking as she continued, *I wasn't wanting to die.*

I told her it was all right, that it was all in the past, but she stopped me.

I was trying to punish you. And to keep you with me. Although how I felt the two could go together escapes me, and she attempted to smile.

I offered to pay for coffee. She would need her money in New York, I said. *Please,* and I made her put her purse away. We talked vaguely about catching up again before she left, both of us knowing we wouldn't, and then we kissed each other on the cheek.

I'm glad I saw you, she said, and I lied as I said that I, too, was glad.

As I watched her walk away, I told myself there had been no point in telling her the truth, in saying that so many of her suspicions had, in fact, been correct; I had never really loved her enough, it was true. Worse still, I had slept with Victoria, kissing her for the first time only three weeks after she moved in, sleeping with her when Greta was working, both of us saying how wrong this was, how it shouldn't go on, both of us looking guiltily at each other whenever Greta went out, both of us promising that this would be the last time, the very last time. But it went on, and on, and, most unforgivable of all, I never really thought about how it would affect Greta, what it would do to her; all I thought about was myself.

There was no denying that Greta's behaviour had been extreme and irrational, there was no denying how difficult she was, but there had always been a core of reality to all that she had believed and that was what I had denied her, that was what I still denied her. After she left, I looked at myself in the window of the cafe and then turned away. I had chosen not to hold out that tiny seed, and say yes, it was there, that canker you always felt did exist, and I am sorry for it, I am truly sorry.

In the years that followed, I lived with Victoria, determined to make it work, to stay with her, because I was ashamed about the way in which I had behaved. Towards the end, she told me I had changed, I was not the person she had fallen in love with; I had become, and she had tried to find the words she needed, *so obsessed with making up for what happened.*

At first I did not understand what she meant. I thought it was my work she was referring to, and it was true I had thrown myself into healing others, leaving little time over for her.

But it was not just that. She felt I had stayed with her to justify the impact our affair had had on Greta. I had stayed with her but I had also never let myself love her.

We've had no joy, she said, and I wanted to hug her, I wanted to deny it, but I couldn't.

I missed her when she left. I still miss her. I do not know what the truth is. It was all so clouded that I could not see anything properly, and I just let her go.

Greta rang me once before she left for New York and I did not return her call. She left her address with the receptionist, who gave it to me, and as I held the paper in my hands, I thought for a moment about just letting it fall in the bin, but then I decided against it. I suppose I thought that one day I might want to contact her. I suppose I hoped I might finally be ready to apologise.

— 5 —

Silas told me that he did not realise that Rudi was seriously ill.

I never really looked at him, he said. *I never noticed anything much about him. It was always her that I was watching. Always.*

Constance was filling a saucepan with rainwater from the tank at the side of the shack, and it was only when she turned towards him that he noticed how drawn her mouth was, how tired her eyes, and he stopped, anxious.

Are you all right? he asked, but she did not reply.

She just nodded towards the stairs, balancing the saucepan in her hands, as he knocked it in his rush to open the door for her.

The smell hit him as soon as he stepped inside. There was no trace of the sweetness that had often overwhelmed him. In its place was a rotten, fetid odour, the staleness of vomit still clotting the air.

He collapsed last night, and she knelt over Rudi who lay, hunched up as a child lies, face down on the mattress.

At first I just thought he was just drunk, Silas told me.

But then he realised it was something else, something worse, and he began to ask her questions without thinking, wanting to know how long Rudi had been in a fever, where he was feeling pain, trying to gather information that he did not know how to use.

Ignoring him, she bent down and turned Rudi carefully. When Silas tried to help her, she only motioned him away, the irritation in her face enough to finally silence him.

It's all right, she whispered to her father, her voice soft and cool as she washed him gently, the precious rainwater trickling over his forehead, his neck, his chest, *it's all right.*

As he watched, Silas felt useless, and he backed away, the smell and the heat of the room only making him ill. Leaning against the window frame, he watched her lift the faded blue singlet Rudi always wore, revealing the skin on his chest, pale and puckered, completely hairless. She continued bathing him, her hands steady and sure as she moved the washer down to where the tumour was, a great lump, purple and angry.

We really should get him to the hospital. Silas heard the alarm in his own voice. *He needs medical help.*

She had a pipette in her hand and she asked her father to open his mouth, just slightly. Silas could see Rudi staring at her, his faded blue eyes focused on her alone as she administered the drops, his dry cracked lips barely open, the struggle to swallow evident.

I can get a four-wheel drive out here, or call the flying doctor.

I would go with you. He knew she was not listening. *Let me do something.*

She gave him the saucepan and pointed to the rainwater tank and he took it from her without another word.

He carted water for her. Back and forth, throughout the length of the day. Breathing in the sweetness of the garden before he had to return to the stench of that room, Silas would sit on the steps for a moment and look across the thick tangle of colour, an abundance of life that seemed even more lurid after the darkness of the shack, and out towards those ranges, huge and still, in the distance.

Rudi would die. Unless she let him go to a hospital, he would die; no matter how cool she kept him, no matter how soothing her words, no matter what drops she was administering. But there was no way Silas could convince her of the need to get outside help.

She told me he had been ill for some time. She said he drank to ease the pain, and Silas looked across at me as he remembered, as he tried to explain.

She had known about the tumour, but the few attempts she had made to broach the subject with her father had been of no use. He was as fit as a bull, he would protest. *Look,* and he would flex his arm to show her muscles he believed still existed. She could neither talk to him about it nor offer any assistance in prescribing treatment.

He could not see himself. She had whispered those words,

not wanting Rudi to hear her doubt in his judgement. *He did not choose the right remedies, and there was nothing I could do.*

By the end of the day, she was clearly exhausted. Dark rings bruised the pale skin under her eyes, and her hands were unsteady as she held the drops to her father's mouth. Silas offered to take over while she slept.

I want to help, he urged.

She looked doubtful.

Please.

One last dose in an hour and then just keep him cool, she instructed.

She cleared the books from where they had been piled on top of the sagging divan and lay down, her black hair silky still like the sea at night, her violet eyes finally closed, her breathing deep and even. Silas just watched her. Barely aware of Rudi, he wanted only to drink in this moment of being able to observe her, unobserved, of being able to let himself sink, deep, into the sight of her stretched out, this close to him.

He realised he must have dozed off after he had given Rudi his drops, parting his lips with the tip of his fingers so that he could insert the pipette, his skin dry like sand, because when he woke, Rudi's eyes were open and he was staring at Silas.

I have failed, and he reached for Silas, trying to draw him closer to the rancid smell that came from his mouth.

Silas shook his head, wanting to calm him as Constance

had done, but he was unable to find the words.

Look what I am leaving her, and Rudi waved his hand aimlessly before it crashed back down to his side.

Silas could see Constance stirring. She was there in the darkness, only feet away. He could lift her hair, its weight falling heavy against his finger and kiss her, her cheek cool beneath his lips. He did not want her to wake and take over, dismissing him as she had done so often before.

Rudi's hand grasped his wrist. His words were a hiss in the quiet. *She does not know the world.*

Silas told him to hush. *This is where she has wanted to be,* his whispered attempt at reassurance falling unheard.

Rudi needed a drink but when Silas offered him water, he only shook his head. *A drink,* he repeated, and although Silas, too, would have liked some of the whisky that he knew Rudi kept next to the stove, he ignored his request.

I didn't want to be alone. When they all went, I didn't want to be alone, and Rudi's words were filled with such self-pity that Silas flinched, the flannel now dripping water onto the floor, trickling between his fingers, as he stared at Rudi in dismay. *When they wanted to take her, I stopped them,* and he turned his head to where Constance was lying, asleep. *All my notes, they are not what I have found, they are her words, they are what she knows. When she was young, I could teach her, I did teach her, and there were others, people who understood our work. Not from there,* and he groaned as he attempted to wave his hand in the direction of the town. *People from the outside world. Now there is no one. She has no one.*

Silas looked over to the divan but he could only just discern her shape, the smooth curve of her, one long arm trailing down to the ground, the velvet of her skin, just her hand, milky white in the light of the moon. When he turned back to Rudi again, his eyes were closed and his forehead felt slightly cooler.

Silas was exhausted. As he stood up slowly, she stirred. Her face was turned in his direction and he could see her eyes glistening in the dark; she was not quite awake and not quite asleep, uncertain in that moment as to who he was and what he was doing there.

He's all right, Silas whispered, wanting only to lie close to her and to feel her healing wholeness.

She turned over.

And not even thinking to ask, he just curled up into the small space next to her, unable to even look at her, as he breathed in the life that emanated from her limbs. With one arm around her, he drew her close, not daring to feel surprise at the lack of resistance in her body, and he buried his face in the darkness of her hair.

Love me, he would have whispered; in fact his mouth was open, ready to form the words, *love me*, a desperate plea that came from such an aching emptiness, but then she turned.

They were almost lilac, her eyes, paler in the moonlight, wide open and remote in their unseeing gaze.

He will be better, and her breath was cold on Silas's cheek as she spoke. *I can heal him.*

How could he tell her that what she believed was impossible? He said nothing, and in that moment, lying there with her, Silas wanted to believe she was right. She could heal Rudi, she could heal him, she could do anything.

— 6 —

Silas took Belladonna for three days, morning, noon and night, the drops sweet underneath his tongue, his eyes closed as he swallowed, his faith uncertain as he waited.

Each day as he walked to the library, the autumn mornings cool and fresh, the grass in the parklands damp beneath his feet, clear diamonds of light sparkling across the harbour, he was aware of a sense of agitation quickening. Because there was, he told me, a whisper of change, tangible, promising, but impossible to hold.

The terrible burning in his heart had not ceased, but when it came, which was infrequently, he no longer doubled over in pain, unable to move. He would feel it drawing in, pulling tighter, and he would brace himself for an unendurable wringing, only to feel immense relief at the slow easing that followed, his breath remaining stable as he realised he would be all right, this time he would be all right, and he would place his hand on his chest, grateful for yet another reprieve, yet unable to see it as anything more than just that, a temporary reprieve.

Silas told me how he had been feeling when we had our next consultation. He also told Greta a day later.

I've been worried about you, he said when he turned up at her apartment early one Friday evening.

It had been two weeks since she had sat opposite him, two weeks since she had told him her story, and she had not seen him since.

I've been, he did not know what the word was, and he drummed his fingers on the door as he searched for it, *anxious, I suppose.*

Her body was blocking the entrance as she told him how busy she had been, *getting everything onto disk,* and her tone was defensive despite the smile. *I would have been in touch.*

She could see he felt awkward trying to conduct this conversation at her door, and as he said he had missed seeing her around, she knew he was hoping to find a welcome in her face that would ease him, but there was only resistance.

I guess that's the way it will be, now that I've almost finished, and she could not look at Silas, not for long.

Later, when she told me how she had greeted him, she said that it was because she felt like such a fool. *And so afraid of liking someone again.*

When Silas asked if he could come in, she stepped back, still without looking at him, telling him she only had a few moments, she had to go out.

He went to sit and then, seeing her face, decided against it.

Can I get you anything? she asked, making a show of gathering together her money, phone and a coat.

Silas just shook his head and for a moment neither of them spoke.

Then he told me, and Greta smiled at the shamelessness of Silas's lie, *that he had a message for me.* She looked at me. *He said you had asked after me, that you wanted to get in touch.*

She remembered how she had been angry with him. She had not understood. She had thought for a moment that he was just being cruel, that it was some kind of joke.

Are you trying to be funny?

No, and he stood up, the hurt on his face now so nakedly obvious that she felt ashamed of her behaviour.

It wasn't the way I had wanted it to be, she told me.

In the silence that followed, she took one step towards him and then stopped. She could see he did not understand her reaction to his presence, and she did not know how to begin to explain.

There was a slight breeze through her window and as the curtain lifted, she attempted to still it, the cloth falling beneath her hands. She heard him take a deep breath, the inhalation of someone trying to find calm, and when she faced him again, he was looking directly at her.

Is it because we talked?

She turned her gaze to the ground.

It wasn't so bad. What you did. Silas's voice was gentle. *Not in the scheme of things.*

She twisted the ring on her finger, still unable to face him, and then she let her hands fall to her side. *Yes it was.*

In the early evening, with the trees swaying against the window, they finally moved towards each other.

I've missed you, and their eyes met. His grin was sheepish as he felt her soften.

With the curtain dancing around them, she could feel his hand on the soft curve of her breast as he unbuttoned her shirt. She was surprised to find she was helping him, her fingers knotted in his, her velvet skin warm against him, her breath sweet and smoky in his mouth, her eyes still on him as she slid her hand into his jeans, rolling them off as she told him that she, too, had missed him, both of them fearing that the other would pull away, that this hold would be broken at any moment.

Later, when her room was dark and the night sky was black outside her window, she asked him if he was going to tell her his story.

What do you mean? He was shivering, suddenly aware of how cold it had become.

Your tale. What happened to you out there.

Silas had moved away from her, despite the fact that she was the only warmth in the cool of that night. He was sitting up now and she realised he was going to go. She could see his clothes illuminated by the street light, lying in a heap on the floor, and he reached for them, the scars on his arm vivid in that one strip of yellow.

As Greta watched him put on his T-shirt, she tried to joke. What he had done couldn't be that bad in the scheme of things. *Honestly,* and she attempted to laugh, suddenly nervous as she realised she did not know if she was, in fact, capable of hearing what she had asked to be told.

Silas couldn't look at her.

With his hands clasped around his arms, he sat with his back turned towards her. It was the ridges in his spine that she stared at, each knot visible through his T-shirt, as he began to speak.

He couldn't face me, she told me later. *Not until he had finished.*

And then he left. Standing by the front door, he made her promise him one thing. *Call him.*

Who? she asked.

Daniel.

Greta said nothing.

I know he would like to hear from you.

She told him to go. She would see him again soon, and under the glare of the corridor lights, he tried to kiss her, but she moved away, closing her front door on him before he had even made it to the lift.

the unknown world

And further, while we were preparing the so-called old medicines we never forgot our position as explorers of the unknown world of results, of effects; never forgetting the ground work of our healing art, we prepared from time to time new medicines also; we made regular provings at least once a year, often twice and even three times a year. These provings were the high feasts in our church, and you cannot consider yourself true members of it without joining in these feasts.

Proving is the most wonderful thing, the world has never known its like. We suffer, and we enjoy it; we sacrifice a little of our comfort, and gain years of strength by it; we go to school to learn, and we increase the certainty of the healing art.

Constantine Hering (1800–1880)

$\sim$ *1* $\sim$

I did not, as Greta had assumed, know the entire story. Silas never told me, and as I filled in the gaps from the little she revealed, I marvelled at the strength with which she had listened to him and chosen not to turn her back. In the end, she was his confessor. He needed someone to be able to hear him and carry the weight of what he believed he had done. He had seen her frailty and he had sensed her strength.

Later, I wondered how I could have failed to realise what had happened. It was all there, every piece laid out in front of me, but I had somehow remained blind to that one essential kernel, unable to see the grain from which it had all grown, until Greta made it clear to me, the morning we met, shortly after I stopped seeing Silas as a patient.

I am not a therapist, I had once told Silas. *If you just want to confess all your crimes and misdemeanors, I may not be the person for you.* And I smiled as I remembered my words.

— 2 —

Silas told me that when he woke the morning after he had nursed Rudi through the night, Constance was still asleep in his arms.

He did not dare breathe, and as he turned slowly, he saw that Rudi was awake, only feet away, and he shifted again, quickly, wanting to go back to the night that had passed, the shimmering darkness of lying awake next to Constance while she slept, no longer even aware of his presence.

But moments later, she, too, realised that Rudi was stirring, and she got up and took his hand, seemingly oblivious to Silas's presence.

It was not until she peeled back the sheet that had covered him that Silas knew she had worked wonders. The tumour was still there but it had receded, the growth definitely smaller than it had been the day before.

Rudi looked at Constance for confirmation and she told him, despite not being able to see the plea in his eyes.

It's a little better, she whispered, and his fingers trembled as he felt for the lump.

It was miraculous, Silas told me. *I was in awe.*

She was standing back from Rudi now, and her eyes were focused. But it was not her father that she was looking at, it was the air around him (*the light, I suppose, the charge,* Silas told me), and Silas, too, tried to see, but there was only that body, stretched out flat in front of him.

I remember thinking that everything I had heard about her was true, that there were no more doubts. She just was, and he looked at the ceiling as he searched for the word, *extraordinary.*

Silas crossed the saltbush flats that led back to town, each of his senses keen to the brilliant blue sky overhead, the soft mauve of the ranges to one side of him, and, on the other, the gulf sparkling beyond the mangrove swamps. He could hear it all, the scratch of the dry twigs against his skin, each footfall in the dirt, the flick of a lizard's tail as it darted away, the quickness of his own breath as he hurried back to the Port, wanting to get the few things she needed so that he could return to her as soon as possible.

It was not until he reached the place where the track turns into the dirt road at the edge of town that he stopped, aware of how rapidly his heart was beating. As the cool morning breeze floated across from the gulf, he remembered the brush of her hair against his cheek, the slight down on the back of her neck, the smooth curve of her hip, all as he had felt them the night before, his body cradled against hers in the darkness, and as he remembered, he shivered, aware, in that moment, of the gulf between night and day.

It was too early for Pearl's to be open, it was too early for anyone to be up, but for the first time since he had arrived, Silas did not find the emptiness of the town unsettling. There was a peace to it, everything was as it should be. Even his mother's house, collapsing into a tangle of weeds and cactuses, no longer looked forlorn; its dilapidation seemed almost graceful.

At Thai's, Eli and Lucas were lying head to toe on the couch, Jade and Sass were curled up at the end of Thai's bed. Silas tiptoed past, letting himself into his cottage, hastily packing the few belongings he would need. As he scribbled a note for Thai, he was not aware that Lucas was awake and watching him from the doorway.

Where are you going? he asked, rubbing the sleep from the corner of his eyes.

Silas looked across at him. *To the garden,* he whispered.

Why?

Silas grinned at him. *Can you keep a secret?*

Lucas nodded, eyes wide as he waited for Silas to tell.

I'm in love, and Silas pinched his cheek.

Yuk, he was smirking, and then as Silas turned to the door, he followed. *Can I come?*

Silas told him to go back to bed, but Lucas ignored him, jumping down off the verandah and chasing him across the dirt yard, past the race track he and Eli had built and out onto the empty road.

Have you kissed her? he asked, running in an attempt to keep up. He was wrinkling his nose in disgust as he waited for an answer. *Well, have you?*

They were at the front of Pearl's now and Silas was dismayed to see the shop was still closed. He looked at his watch and hesitated for a moment before banging on the window.

Across the road, Mick was opening the garage. He heaved the roller-door up, the clatter of steel making Silas jump. Lucas was pulling on his sleeve, still wanting a response to his question. Silas pushed him away, wishing he had kept quiet, but in that brief moment all he had wanted was to speak, to roll out the deliciousness of the secret so that he could marvel at it, and Lucas had been there.

Silas is in love, the boy chanted, skipping around him, his voice ringing out clear and loud in the stillness of the morning.

Silas knocked on the window again, willing to incur the wrath of Pearl if it meant he could get away from Lucas and out to Constance sooner. From inside he could hear her opening the door that led to the rooms at the back, the rooms where she was born, where she had always lived and where she would die.

Silas knocked again, and he could hear her calling out,

Hold your horses, as she moved slowly, rolling on fat ankles, towards the front door.

Did you stick your tongue in? Lucas was pulling on the hem of his shirt now, and as he turned around to tell him to shut up, he'd had enough, he saw Mick cross the road, making his way towards them.

Leaning awkwardly on his crutches, he was attempting to step onto the island that cut the main road in two, a thin strip of gravel decorated with the hideous palms that had been planted by the Port Tremaine Local Action Group over ten years ago.

Silas is in love, Lucas shouted out, but Mick did not say a word.

Silas watched as Mick struggled with the crutches, trying to get a hold in the gravel, staring at him the whole time. He was about to ask if he needed a hand, but the expression on Mick's face silenced him. He did not know what it was that he was coming over to say, but he did not want to hear it; not on this perfect morning, not now.

As Pearl drew the bolts, pushing the heavy wooden doors to the shop open, Mick stepped down onto the other side of the road and stopped.

What's the racket? She had her arms folded across her stained nightgown, and her glasses balanced at the end of her nose.

Silas told her Rudi had been ill and he needed to get some supplies up to them.

Probably just drank too much, and she snorted derisively. *Anyone would have thought the town was on fire with that carry-on.*

It was incredible, and Silas recounted the story of Rudi's miraculous recovery as he filled his arms with what seemed to be the most practical items he could find: candles, matches, tea, sugar, bread, even a few cans of soup; the list Constance had given him having been forgotten on his walk back from her place.

Pearl opened a bag of Minties, unwrapping one as she listened to his tale.

Hmph, and she began to add up his purchases. *Sounds like that faith-healing stuff to me.* She leant a little closer. *Did she lay her hands on him?*

Silas had no idea what she had done, but he had seen the change that had occurred, the feat she had performed, and he just wanted to get back to her, to be out there with her again.

In the glare of the morning, Mick had not moved. He was leaning on his crutches and his eyes were on Silas as soon as the screen door banged shut behind him. Lucas was sitting on the kerb, flicking pieces of gravel at the squat trunks of the palms, the constant thwack of the stone against wood loud and irritating in the stillness. He jumped up as soon as he saw Silas, wanting to follow, bounding around him as he made his way over to where Mick waited.

Silas did not know why he went over. Brushing the flies from his face, he wished he hadn't, and he opened his mouth to speak, to ask if there was any problem, but Mick's words silenced him.

Is she all right? He was kicking at the gutter and his face was hard.

Silas did not know who he was talking about.

Well, is she?

Silas could see his own face reflected in Mick's black glasses, that was all he could see, and he did not understand.

Who? and in the instant he asked the question, he knew the answer.

Constance.

Your girlfriend, Lucas giggled, *your girlfriend,* and in his confusion Silas shouted at Lucas, telling him to *shut the fuck up*, his voice louder than he had intended, harsh enough to silence him, so that in the sudden quiet that descended, the three of them just stood there on that empty main street, with Constance's name still hanging between them, heavy, in that hot, still air.

~ *3* ~

Following the instructions Steve had given me, I went out to the edge of town, and as I looked at the miles of flat scrub in front of me, the tufts of saltbush coarse and bare, battered low under the cold winter sky, I knew that this was the way Silas had walked, despite the absence of a discernible track. With the stones sharp against the soles of my shoes, the bare branches scratching my arms, and the constant buzz of flies around my face, I remembered how he had told me that he had run out here, the few things he had bought stuffed into his backpack, the straps cutting into his shoulders, the swing of the weight jarring his limbs as he raced across the hot sandy soil.

He was agitated, the full implications of Mick's concern for Constance's wellbeing seemingly just out of reach. *But the truth is I didn't want to know, I didn't want to see what had become so glaringly obvious,* and as he had told Greta everything, that night in her room, he had scratched at one of the sores on his arm, tearing the wound open without even noticing.

Constance had given him the key to the gate and he had let himself in, fumbling with the lock in his haste to be back there with her, dropping his bag to the ground as he tried to close it again, all that he had brought spilling out across the dirt; his clothes, the tins of food, the matches, gathered together again with twigs, stones and leaves caught up amongst it all.

He was out of breath when he got to her. His mouth was dry from the quick drink he had downed when he was back in the cottage, the alcohol searing his throat as he had swallowed it hastily. His hands were shaking. He pushed the door open, his heart too loud, the clatter of the bag as he dropped it to the ground causing her to shush him with her finger to her lips.

I cannot begin to describe the relief I felt at seeing her, and he had leant forward and put his head in his hands, while Greta had listened.

It was all right, he told himself. She was as remarkable as she had been when he left her only hours earlier, and he just stood, leaning against the door of the shack, staring at her.

When she spoke, he jumped at the sound of her voice. It was a remedy she wanted. The doors to the cabinet were open, the rows of brown bottles, each labelled, arranged across the shelves, all within her reach. When she told him the name of the one that she needed, he almost laughed.

But you know where it is. He did not understand. He knew

she could see them, far more clearly than he could. She could work miracles. She did not need his assistance, and he did not move to help her.

Can you get it, please? She was irritated now, and stung by the hardness of her tone, he searched for the name on the label, finally handing it to her, thinking that perhaps this was some kind of a joke that was lost on him. But if it was, she wasn't smiling.

All morning he followed her orders. Food needed preparing, water needed fetching, wood chopping, sheets washing; he did it all as soon as she asked, trying not to think of Mick's comment, trying not to think of Mick at all, but he kept stealing glances at her, knowing he was judging her, assessing her with each sharp doubt that pricked his consciousness, knowing that Mick's presence was still right there with him, despite his efforts to deny it.

It was not until late afternoon that he stopped, his body weak from tiredness, his head overwhelmed. While Rudi slept, he sat under the shade of the peppercorn tree and rolled a cigarette. Constance was watering the garden and in the intensity of the last light it seemed that each petal, each stamen, each leaf, was sparkling, glittering and alive. He watched as she bent over the giant heads of the belladonna, and holding the blossoms in the palms of her open hands, she drank in the perfume, rubbing the petals against her lips.

Why do you do that? he asked, and she straightened, startled.

They revive me, she told him, and she turned back to the plants.

He tried to walk quietly towards her, not wanting her to hear him, just wanting to know if she would see his approach and stop him, or if he would be able to put his arms around her and rest his head against the smooth curve of her shoulder as he longed to. She stepped back at the first sound of his footfall.

What are you doing? she asked. *Why are you creeping up on me?*

You do see me, he said, more out of hope than certainty.

She just pressed the tips of her fingers into her eyelids, shutting her eyes, her mouth drawn tight in pain.

What is it that you see? he asked. *How did you know? How could you do what you did?* and he nodded in the direction of the shack where Rudi lay.

It was not a miracle, and she shook her head slowly. *I just do what he has taught me to do.*

She turned away again, and Silas stared at the graceful curve of her neck, her pale skin dappled in the light. He could not bear it. It was all slipping away, sliding like dirt, and he wanted to stop it, but each time he attempted to, everything jarred, everything was wrong.

He asked after you.

She did not move.

When I was in town. He wanted to know if you were all right.

The flower she had been holding fell to the ground, the white petals spread open on the soil.

Mick?

Mick. It was Silas who repeated his name, *Mick*, the single syllable harsh as he uttered it just one more time for good measure: *Mick.*

And then neither of them said a word, there in the corner of the garden where the weeds were far thicker than he had ever noticed and the thistles were forcing their way through the sagging fence, and for the first time since he had stepped inside that place, the flies were thick against his face and he didn't even attempt to brush them away.

Why hasn't he come?

When she finally spoke, he wanted to block his ears.

Where has he been?

He had heard Pearl's stories about her. He had seen the wonder of her with his own eyes and that was the truth, but when he eventually glanced across at her, she was staring blankly at him, desperate, her eyes unseeing, the dirt smeared across her cheek as she wiped her face with the back of her hand and waited for an answer to her question.

Don't look at me, she told him, and she shook her head. *He knows me, far more than you ever have,* and her stare was defiant. *He sees me for what I am.*

When I remember how Silas tried to explain, how none of it made sense, I wonder at how I failed to grasp what quickly became clear to Greta when she, too, finally heard his story.

It did not take long, Silas told me. From the moment she stepped on the snake, to when she began to be ill.

And I didn't know what to do, he said. *I was helpless.*

But it was not simply a matter of failing to get help in time. Of course it wasn't.

In the darkness of Greta's room, with his face turned towards the wall, he had told her that it had all happened so quickly that he just did not know whether he had seen the snake slithering through the dry and scraggly grass. Perhaps he had been aware of it glittering, its scales coppery in the light, as it had flicked and darted through the dirt; perhaps he had watched, fascinated, as it had slid, stealthy, silent, across the warmth of the stone bench, its eyes two sleepy jewels, its tongue flicking out and then in, and he had wanted to know, for one horrible instant, just exactly what Constance was.

Look out, he should have warned. *Be careful,* he should have said.

But Pearl had told him she was born with venom in her veins and Rudi had told him she could see, *far more than you or I could ever comprehend.*

He had told himself she was all they said and more.

And now there was this, the very presence of Mick there between them, the jagged sharpness of his jealousy enough to spur Silas on, daring him to test all he had wanted to believe.

I wanted it to be true, he had whispered, finally making himself utter the words out loud, to recognise it at last. *I wanted proof.*

And in that one brief moment he had acted in a way that had no sanity, no rationality; he had clung, desperate, to his own ludicrous vision, wanting to believe she would see that snake as it had slithered across her path, right there where her foot was about to land, even if all she saw was just the colours that surrounded it; or that it would slide over her, without harming her; or perhaps, most impossible of all, that even if its venom did slip through her veins it would be like blood on blood, a joining of like with like. Was that what he had done, or had he, as he had tried so hard to believe, seen nothing at all?

Silas told me that she had become sick so quickly.

Let me help you, he had begged.

Pushing him away, shoving him away, she had asked him to leave her, to leave her and her father in peace, and he had said he would do anything, anything at all. What did she need? What should he get for her?

With her mouth twisted in pain, she had vomited on the ground at his feet and told him he had done enough, enough, and all the doubts about himself had solidified, hard and cold inside him, as he saw the look on her face.

She knew, and Greta had just stared at his back. *She saw the worst in my heart, the fact that I had wanted to test her. In whatever way it was that she saw, she saw.*

How could you? she had hissed. *How could you?*

He had told her she needed help, he would be back, and he had run, racing across the hot red plains, stumbling across boulders, tripping on branches that grew lopsided out of the sand; he had not stopped, wanting only to reach the town and call for someone who would know what to do.

It took them an hour to get there, and when they did, she was dead. They told me she'd had an unusually strong reaction to the venom, that some people do.

He had been going to go back, to be with her until someone came. He had made it halfway out there, and then he had remembered the way in which she had looked at him, all that she had accused him of, and his courage had failed him.

I just couldn't face her. I went back to my car and I left.

He had heard the news from the side of the road, somewhere out on the highway, the hot evening air thick around him, his hands shaking as he had attempted to roll a joint, waiting to be put through to the doctor.

He had let the phone fall to the ground.

He had let the match burn to his fingers.

They said there was nothing I could have done.

In the silence, Greta had searched for words. She had remembered the way in which she had once tried to punish me, the worst she had ever done, and she had searched for words.

When he had finally turned to face her, she had reached for him, but he had not taken her hands.

Can you see why I am like this? he had asked her. *Can you see now?* And he had held out his arms, bare under the light, before turning to gather the rest of his clothes.

She had told him that she could, that she understood, swallowing deeply as she spoke, the entire weight of his story there inside her, needing to be digested before she could look him in the eye again, because that was what she wanted, to face him, knowing all that she knew, and to see that he was still the Silas she had slowly come to love.

~ *4* ~

That was the night Silas knew he wanted to go back.

Later he told me that he had not gone home. Knowing he would not be able to sleep (and it was not fear at what sleep could bring but a strange nervous release that kept him awake), he walked up and down the cold winter streets, staring into shop windows, stopping in bars, eventually ending up at an all-night cafe he used to frequent on his regular drunken nights out.

He took a table right at the back, where he was almost lost in the folds of the faded red curtains that acted as a door leading to a dingy outdoor toilet used by junkies to shoot up, and he ordered a coffee.

The woman at the table next to him was nodding off. The cigarette in her hand was burning down, unsmoked, the tip dangerously close to both her chipped fingernails and her long, peroxided hair. He leant over, trying to slip it from her grasp without disturbing her, but she jumped, starting at his touch.

What the fuck do you want? Her words were thick and slurred.

Silas told her he hadn't wanted her to burn herself.

She stared at him through mascara-smudged eyes for a moment and then smiled, the sly, lazy smile of someone who has floated away from the world, adrift in a better place.

I know you, she said.

He was about to tell her that he didn't think she did, but then he realised she may have seen him here, years ago, or in one of the other places he used to go to.

Yeah, and she was grinning as she nodded at him, clearly remembering something that amused her.

Where from? Silas lit a cigarette from the end of hers, curious now.

Her eyes narrowed a little further as she leant forward to examine him more closely, swaying slightly as she did so.

I reckon we fucked, and the smile on her face was sly as she said his name, *Silas.*

The cafe was dark. With only a single light, shaded by a bubbled yellow glass ball, it was impossible to see anyone too clearly, unless they were right there, in your face, but even that proximity would probably only lend a distortion of its own. Silas didn't recognise her, but he couldn't dismiss her claim as impossible.

She was still looking at him, shaking her head, the last of the ash from her cigarette finally crumbling into the brittle petals of the plastic roses on the table.

What happened to you? She leant a little closer, almost falling off her seat as she did so.

He turned back to his coffee, the bitterness of each sip settling uncomfortably into his stomach, when she spoke again.

What's this? She was pointing at his arm, the fact that her question had remained unanswered only just having registered.

Silas told her he had got into a fight.

Yeah? She peered so closely at the scars, Silas felt the brush of her hair, the ends brittle and dry, along his skin.

With myself, he added, not sure why he was giving her this extra detail without having been asked for it.

When it came, her laugh was raspy, and as she opened her mouth, the smear of lipstick cracked at the corners of her lips leaving dry flakes of red clinging to her skin, and Silas could see that her teeth were rotten; the holes were visible, even in the darkness of that room.

No shit, she finally said, her eyes narrowing. There was a cunningness now as she sized him up. *Got a few bucks you could lend us? For another coffee?*

Silas gave her what he had, which wasn't much, but clearly far more than she had expected. When he left, she was still looking at the fifty-dollar note, turning it over in her hands, before glancing back at him, quickly, furtively, uncertain as to whether he had made a mistake and would turn back and snatch it from her.

As he walked down the street at the back of the cafe, skirting the bulging garbage bags and wheelie bins filled to overflowing, he wondered at her story. He did not like to think he could have had that level of intimacy with someone and be left with no memory of the event.

Standing outside Greta's block of flats, he looked up to the darkness of her window for a moment and then turned towards home.

He had spoken. He had never thought he would, but he had, and he was exhausted now. In an hour or so it would be morning. The few people who were still out would stumble onto the streets, their faces ashen, the brilliant colours in which they had adorned themselves fading in the coldness of the dawn, the trees shivering with the freshness of the early breeze, the first light grey and unforgiving in that brief moment before the sun began to warm the sky.

He let himself into his apartment and turned on all the lights. The piles of paper, the attempts at categorising himself, were still stacked in boxes by the front door. He could not remember how many bundles he had made. It did not matter.

It was when he was sitting in the leather armchair that had once belonged to his father that he realised his vague thoughts of returning to Port Tremaine were no longer just a possible course of action to consider. He wanted to see Rudi, he wanted to at least try to explain.

I need to face him, he told me when he saw me next, and when, once again, I failed to understand the need he had to atone for a wrong that still made no sense to me, I asked him why he felt this was necessary.

With his face turned towards the door, he just said that he needed to apologise, to say he was sorry, and he did not explain any further.

— 5 —

When Greta received her second-last payment for the work she had done, she realised she finally had enough money to go to New York.

This was what she had wanted, she told me, for as long as she could remember, but now that it could actually happen, she felt uncertain. She booked the ticket before she lost her nerve and rang her friend who had moved there some months ago, knowing she would only encourage her to go.

But I haven't paid yet, she said.

Well, make sure you do it.

And she promised her that she would.

Each day, she thought about ringing Silas, or even visiting him. She would let him know of her decision and he would be pleased for her, he would tell her she should go, and they would look at each other, his slightly wolfish mouth twisted into an embarrassed smile as she told him that it was all right, they were aware of the worst in each other and it was all right. But days passed and she still hadn't picked up the phone or stopped off at his apartment. She just wasn't ready. She wanted to be, but she wasn't.

Late one afternoon, as she was walking back from the final meeting with the academic for whom she had been working, she paused, as she always did, at the intersection leading to Silas's street, and then turned towards his building without giving herself a moment to change her mind.

The front doors were open, as was the door to his flat. A woman in a dark grey suit, her blonde hair piled up in a French knot, stood at the entrance with a folder in one hand.

You're here to look at the apartment? she asked, passing Greta an application form.

I'm actually here to see the owner, Greta told her.

Through the doorway, she caught a glimpse of several couples, opening cupboards, looking into rooms, the women's heels loud on the parquetry floor, the men nodding in agreement as their partners expressed their approval at various aspects of the place.

It will be furnished? one woman asked.

That's what I gather, the real estate agent said.

Greta had not been to Silas's apartment since the night she had stayed with him. She had a dim recollection of the size of the place, but she was still surprised by how large it seemed, how grand the furniture was.

Obviously the clutter will be cleared, and the agent smiled as she pointed to the boxes stacked in one corner of the hall.

Has Silas gone? Greta asked her. *The owner?*

The woman looked across at her briefly. *I believe he goes in a couple of weeks. That's when the place becomes vacant,* and she took an application form from one of the men.

I'm very interested, he told her.

Someone else pressed another form into her hand. Three women waited with forms and references ready to hand over.

We all are, one of them said, clearly irritated at the man's assumption that first in would lead to first served.

Greta left. Outside in the cool of the evening, the street lights were coming on, flickering for a moment, spilling a white light across the pavement. She turned towards home.

She was surprised he had not told her of his decision to leave, and as she admitted to herself that she was also hurt, she knew she didn't just want to let him know of her own imminent departure.

She remembered Silas standing at her door, ready to flee, and as he had turned to go, he had urged her once again to try to make amends with the past. She did not know he had been lying when he had told her that I wanted to talk to her, and she wanted to know what it was, exactly, that I had supposedly said when I had mentioned I would like to see her again.

I wanted to be sure, she explained, *that you did want to hear from me.*

Catching a glimpse of herself in a shop window, her cheeks flushed from the cold, she told herself it was time she just did it. She would ring tonight, as soon as she got upstairs.

6

The last remedies that I prescribed for Silas were Cactus Grandiflorus and Lachesis. I wished him well as I gave them to him and I urged him to contact me if he felt the slightest need.

So that's it? he asked.

For now, and I smiled at him. *But who knows? We clear up one thing and another surfaces.*

He had told me that it had now been almost six weeks since he had hurt himself.

And the heart? I had asked.

Silas had placed his hand on his chest.

Still there?

He had grinned as he had told me that the pains had not completely gone. *It is like it is always pulled a little too tight. But it is not nearly as bad as it was.*

Anything else?

He had been about to tell me that there wasn't, but then he had hesitated. He had said that the sensation was barely worth mentioning, that it didn't really trouble him, he simply found it strange.

It is like a constant pins and needles, he had said. *In my upper body. As though there is electricity short-circuiting.*

And this is new, this sensation?

It wasn't, but it had seemed so insignificant with all that followed that Silas had never thought to mention it before. It had bothered him from when he had first arrived in Port Tremaine, and then it had gone, shortly after he had left.

This is what happens, I had told him, and I had explained about an illness returning to its source before cure.

He had been surprised when I had wanted to give him the additional remedies. *What you've done so far is pretty miraculous,* he had said, glancing over to the piece of paper on which I was writing.

It's not a question of miracles, and we had both stood up. *It's just what I have been trained to do.*

As we said goodbye in reception, I repeated my instructions to him. *The Cactus Grandiflorus first, and then, if there's no improvement, the Lachesis.*

Which is? he asked.

Snake.

He did not want to look at me.

It will help, I said and I wished him well.

As he turned to the door, one hand on the knob, he stopped for a moment. *I just hope I have the courage.*

He was referring to his decision to return, and as I

watched him leave, I, too, hoped he would find the strength he would need, although I was still unaware as to the extent of what it was that he felt he needed to confront.

Each time he dreamt of Constance, Silas saw her as he had made her up to be. There she was, impossibly beautiful, the glossy sheen of her hair startling against her ivory skin, her lips too red and soft, her violet eyes fringed by soot-black lashes and her head bent low and graceful, with the petals of that flower spread open in her hands.

He would wake, stunned by the vision. It was usually the early hours of the morning, the darkness tinged with enough grey to let him know he had left night behind, and he would stay completely still, not daring to move as the dream dissolved, disintegrating like ash between his fingers, aware of his desire to tear at his own flesh and the need to resist it.

He did not know how he had done what he had done. He could not comprehend what kind of a person he must have been to act as he had acted and, appalled, he would feel the poison of what he had been, and what he felt he therefore still was, seeping viscous, spreading like tar, bitter and black, from his chest, through his stomach, his limbs; all of him sinking with its weight.

He remembered when he had first decided to travel out to Port Tremaine and it was as though he was remembering another person in another life. Recalling the great flurry with which he had cloaked his departure, the impossible romantic vision of it, made him flinch because he knew the fear he had been trying to hide.

He had stayed awake the night before he made that trip, while Tess Davis had slept, drunkenly sprawled across his bed, and he had smoked joint after joint in an attempt to come down from the speed that had left his jaw tense, his mouth dry and his hands incapable of remaining steady. He had sat in front of the window, alarmed that he could not see his own reflection each time he lit another match, the flame flaring bright in the darkness, and in his paranoid out-of-it state, he had thought that perhaps he did not exist.

Am I here? he had asked Tess, shaking her awake.

She had looked at him for a brief moment and then closed her eyes again.

In the morning, when he had been convincing her to come with him, he had told her that he loved her, and he had truly believed his words. He had imagined them setting up a life together. He had told her how amazing it would be, what adventures they would have, and she had smoked a cigarette and just nodded in response, her eyes wide and dazed.

This time, the fear Silas felt was not hidden.

Standing in the street with the leaves crisp around his feet, he rang Greta's buzzer three times. He was folding the note he had written when he saw her, tall and beautiful under the rawness of the clear blue sky, striding towards him, one hand raised in greeting, and there was both defiance and hesitation in the gesture.

They kissed awkwardly, neither of them able to fix their gaze on the other, and she asked him up.

I was going to come and see you earlier, Silas said.

She sat on the bed, on the other side of the room, and just looked at him as she rolled a cigarette, leaving him stumbling for words.

I'm sorry, he told her, *about the other night.*

Why? she asked.

About just going the way I did.

She licked the paper flat and lit a match, giving it one sharp flick to extinguish the flame. As she inhaled, she crossed her legs, tucking her feet in. She was agitated, it was there in the straightness of her back, the slight twitching of her leg, the sharp tap of her cigarette against the ashtray.

Why did you do it? she asked him and her voice was suddenly harder than it had been.

He thought, for one awful moment, that she was referring to all that he had told her and she saw the realisation cross his face, the sudden desire to just leave, the mistake he had made in coming to see her, all there, naked in its terror as he stood up, knocking the edge of her desk, sending her papers flying across the floor.

I'm not talking about that, she said.

He did not know what she meant.

Why did you pretend that Daniel wanted to hear from me?

He did not know what to say. He had been wanting to help, to do something good, and as he tried to explain, she could see that he, too, did not understand why he had lied in the way he had.

Did you speak to him? he asked her.

She nodded.

Was it all right?

She turned to the window and her expression was blank as she said she had made the call. *Yesterday evening,* and she jerked her head as though to indicate that the recent past sat only just behind her on the bed.

And? Silas asked.

We're having a coffee. In a couple of days.

Silas watched as she got up and washed out the ashtray under the tap, talking with her back to him. *I wish you hadn't lied.*

But you don't hate me for what I did? Silas asked.

She did not answer for a moment, and her voice was hesitant when she finally spoke. *I don't like it and I don't understand you, but I don't hate you.*

And he had to turn his back to her, he had to stare out the window across the tops of the trees trembling in the breeze as he alluded to the story he had told her, and the decision he had subsequently made.

I wondered whether you were ever going to let me know, and she explained how she had been to his flat.

I have to at least try to see him, he said. *I may not do it, but I have to try.*

And you'll be gone for a while?

He told her he didn't think so, and her eyes narrowed in disbelief.

That's what they all say, and she attempted to laugh.

Sitting opposite her in the cafe where we met, I could see she wished she had been able to show more feeling at the time, but she had only come towards reaching a peace with all he had told her now that he was gone.

Sometimes I think that he was just deluded, that he had simply imagined he saw the snake, and she played with a sachet of sugar, rolling it in the palms of her hands, *and afterwards, when she was bitten, he hated the part of him that had, for one instant, watched, fascinated, wanting to know what she was; so much so that he thought he caused it all, somehow. I mean, it would all have been so quick, how could he have stopped it?*

She squinted slightly, as she looked up to the brightness of the sky.

Other times I am not so sure. He wanted to test her, and in one of those terrible moments he did the wrong thing, the completely wrong thing.

I recalled the pain that Silas had inflicted upon himself, and I looked away, not wanting to answer the question that I knew she was asking as I told her that I didn't know where the truth lay.

She closed her eyes. *We are all capable of desiring the very worst for another.* She put the sugar back in the bowl. *And we are all capable of doing what we think we would never be capable of doing.*

And as I remembered holding Victoria, desperately wanting the sweet wholeness of her body only hours after leaving Greta alone in that ambulance, I told the waiter that we were fine, that we didn't want anything else, that we were about to go.

— *8* —

Silas left, I know that much. His apartment was rented out and he was gone. Walking past his door one afternoon, I glanced at the names at the entrance and saw that his had been taped over. After I had heard all that Greta had to say, I had finally understood why he had needed to return, and why he had been so anxious at the thought, and I had found myself wondering, daily, whether he had actually taken the steps he had been hoping to take, and whether he was all right.

About a month after I passed his apartment, I first heard about this proving and about six weeks after that, I made my decision to come here, taking the turn-off to Port Tremaine on my way out to this house, wanting to see it all for myself and wanting to find out whether he had returned.

Now, four weeks later, we are about to commence.

This morning Jeanie and I took Sam for a walk to the pre-Cambrian gorge about a mile from here. We did not talk for most of the way, the force of the wind was too strong to hear anything, and with our heads bent low, we made our way in silence to where the rocks lean at different angles to reveal the ages, their surfaces smooth and cold to the touch.

In shelter from the wind, we stopped to sit on a fallen tree, both of us taking our time before we chose to speak, neither of us wanting to break the purity of the silence.

Are you glad you came here?

Her question made me start slightly, the rupture of the quiet and the reality of the task we are about to embark on bringing me back from my thoughts. It will be a long process (this is only the first of many stages), and whether or not my involvement will continue until the end will depend on the reaction that both Larissa and Matthew have to the remedy, after they begin taking it tomorrow. If they do exhibit symptoms, if their vibration rates closely align with that of the substance we are proving, they will be selected for further testing once we return to the city, and there will be yet another culling before those who continue go on to be given a third, and even higher, dose.

But despite the fact that it will be many months before we can even begin to see the whole picture, and even though it is impossible to know where this process will lead us or what our involvement will be, I am glad to be a part of it, and as I told Jeanie this, I was surprised to suddenly realise that I did feel considerably lighter than I had when I arrived.

And the other stuff? Jeanie waved her hand in the direction of Port Tremaine.

I dropped a piece of shale I had been holding, letting it fall into the small pool of brown rainwater that had collected at the base of the tree, and as the surface was disturbed I became aware of the perfect reflection it had contained – my own face looking back at me and, beyond, the sharpness of the winter blue sky.

You mentioned about going out to Rudi's, and she shaded her eyes against the glare as she watched what appeared to be an eagle, the whoosh of its wings stirring the stillness.

I wanted to know whether he went back. We both stood, turning towards the path that would take us out to the plains.

And did he?

I reached down to stroke Sam, picking up the stick she had dropped and holding it absentmindedly in my hands.

No one knew. Or rather, no one told me, and I smiled as I remembered the attempts I had made to find out.

Not even Pearl, the one person who I had hoped would help, had revealed anything of any substance. As I had peered through the flyscreen, her face cut into a myriad of tiny squares, I had realised almost immediately that it was foolish to expect a direct answer; I had sensed it as she took off her glasses and rubbed them against the sleeve of her nightgown. She had looked straight at me, my gaze held by her own, as she had tried to work out a story, something, anything to keep me there with her, a rare distraction from the relentless tedium of another day.

I've heard he was seen, but I can't say I ever laid eyes on him.

Who saw him? I had asked, wanting something more definite.

People round about.

Anyone I could talk to?

She had put her glasses back on. *Can't remember their names. Seems no reason why he wouldn't have come my way. If he was here, that is.*

So you don't think he was here?

She had scratched at a bite, a red welt on the loose flesh around her wrist. *I don't think I said that,* and she had sniffed to emphasise her point, *did you hear me say that?*

As I relayed the conversation to Jeanie, she laughed, the fierceness of the wind carrying the sound away from us almost immediately, and it seemed, for an instant, that we were going to just slip back into the comfortable silence we had chosen on the way out here, our heads bent low against the force of the weather. But then she stopped, holding me back with the touch of her hand.

What do you think? she asked, and I could see she was genuinely curious.

I looked out across the plains, to the high tops of the ranges that are always within sight, visible from every street of Port Tremaine, changing colour hourly, their presence a constant reminder that life will continue, even as another town dies, and I told her that I didn't know.

I hope he went back. I would like to think he did.

But as we made our way towards the house, I realised it really didn't matter. In simply reaching the point of wanting to return he had come a long way, and if the next stage took more time, then so be it. And as for whether all that he had described for me had ever existed, I did not know; I would probably never know. Because when I found Rudi's place, I saw that what had remained of the garden was now overgrown and untended, whatever bloom there had been had long since faded, and that it was simply impossible to tell whether the vision that Silas had described had ever existed. Dry husks of flowers hung limply from dead branches, paths were made impenetrable by lantana, and in the centre of it all, what was left of the shack no longer resembled a dwelling. Even the fence was in ruins. It leant like some sagging tired beast, great stretches swaying gently in the breeze, other parts still attempting to remain upright despite the weeds that gripped and tugged, pulling each strand of wire back down to the earth.

I walked around the side of that shack, because that was where Steve had told me it would be; her grave, just as he had described. The wooden cross had collapsed and the mound of earth was covered in weeds. But it was not entirely uncared for. There were flowers, the pale belladonna she had loved, the soft sheen on their petals like wax, the fine yellow veins delicate against the cream.

I reached down to touch them and I realised that they had not been laid there as I had thought. They were growing, growing out of the earth in which she had been buried, the only flower left in the garden Silas had told me about, and as I held one in my hands, I breathed in the sweetness, rich and full in the biting cold of the winter air.

I carried that flower with me, all the way across the plains, to where my car waited at the edge of the town, and I rested its tip in a water bottle, hoping it would survive the three-hour journey up to the house, hoping it would stay, miraculously, alive; an emblem of all that Silas had wanted to believe.

It is still there, in a glass next to my bed, resting on top of the scrap of paper with Greta's address written on it. Last night I took it out of the water, the petals long since closed, the bloom discoloured, the stem dripping onto the ink, and I held it, certain for a moment, that I could still smell that sweetness. With my eyes closed, I breathed deeply, wanting to drink it in, wanting to hold it before it faded, and it was not until moments later that I realised there was, in fact, no scent.

I had been remembering.

S O U R C E S

Clarke, John Henry, *A Dictionary of Practical Materia Medica*, Shobi Offset Press 1900.

Hahnemann, Samuel, *Organon of Medicine*, fifth edition.

Hering, Constantine, *The Guiding Symptoms of our Materia Medica.*

Krippner, S. and Rubin, D. (eds), *The Kirlian Aura*, Anchor, New York, 1974. Reproduced in Vithoulkas, George, *The Science of Homeopathy.*

Vithoulkas, George, *The Science of Homeopathy*, B Jain Publishers PVT Ltd, New Delhi, 1980.

Whitmont, Edward C, *Psyche and Substance: Essays on Homeopathy in the Light of Jungian Psychology,* M D North Atlantic Books Homeopathic Educational Services, Berkeley, Cal, 1980, 1991 ed, reproduced with the permission of North Atlantic Books, Berkeley, California, USA.

Every effort has been made to contact the copyright holders of material reproduced in this book and the publishers would welcome any further information.

Printed in Great Britain
by Amazon

82456173R10171